Black Diamond 3:

Lucky Chance

Black Diamond 3:

Lucky Chance

Brittani Williams

www.urbanbooks.net

Urban Books, LLC
97 N18th Street
Wyandanch, NY 11798

ISBN 13: 978-1-60162-651-6
ISBN 10: 1-60162-651-7

First Mass Market Printing March 2015
First Trade Paperback Printing January 2013
Printed in the United States of America

10 9 8 7 6 5 4 3 2 1

Distributed by Kensington Publishing Corp.
Submit Orders to:
Customer Service
400 Hahn Road
Westminster, MD 21157-4627
Phone: 1-800-733-3000
Fax: 1-800-659-2436

Black Diamond 3:

Lucky Chance

A novel by

Brittani Williams

Prologue

Where It All Began

2006

"Why are you staring at me like that, Kemp?" Diamond asked, smiling while admiring her future paycheck. Kemp was fine, but the zeros in his bank account were much more attractive. She'd waited her whole life for the type of life that he could provide and she considered her future with him signed, sealed, and delivered at this point. She smiled, thinking about the glamour that would come along with being his permanent arm piece. For Diamond, snagging him was just as rewarding as a college degree.

"What, I can't admire my *Diamond* now?" he replied, taking a quick bite of his porterhouse steak.

After taking a sip of her red wine she returned to smiling. "I didn't say that. I'm just not used to you admiring me this way that's all."

"Well, I guess it's time for a change. You belong to me, right?"

"No question. I'm here to stay. This Diamond is yours forever." She sat up tall in the chair.

"Now that's what I like to hear, and, since we're on this topic of diamonds being forever, can you tell me the difference between a diamond and a rock or a pebble?" he asked, grabbing hold of her hand with seriousness written all across his face.

"You mean like an alley rock or a pebble?"

"Yes," he quickly replied with a laugh.

"Well, we're priceless, unlike the rest, but you knew that already," she replied confidently.

"Yeah, I see that." He paused and looked around the table to glance at her size-eight frame. "But the thing that makes you so priceless is time. That's the difference."

"Time?" she asked, confused.

"Yes, baby, time. The time it takes to find a precious stone like you compared to any other washed-up rock or pebble is measureless. One would have to damn near slave to find a diamond, which takes time, patience, dedication, loyalty, and hard work to discover. Would you agree?"

"I do." She smiled at his poetic words. She never expected him to say anything so beautiful.

"You do, do you?" he asked with the sexiest smile that Diamond had ever seen on a man. Though she didn't have any intention of falling in love with him, she realized at that moment that she might not be able to avoid it.

"Yes, babe, I do." She leaned across the table and kissed him slowly.

While kissing Diamond he pulled out a ring from his pocket and slipped it on her finger. "What about now?"

"What are saying, Kemp?" she screamed, looking at the huge four-karat diamond ring that he'd placed on her finger.

Kemp signaled the waiter for a bottle of champagne. "I believe I've already said it."

"But it's only been six weeks," she said while looking down at the ring, which sparkled with the slightest movement.

"Listen to me, Diamond; there are only two types of lovers in the world. You have those who believe that love comes in time and then you have my type—who believes that time comes with love. Which one are you?"

"The one that comes with you," she said excitedly.

"I thought you'd say that." He smiled.

"So when, Kemp?" she asked with a giggle. She'd almost reached the finish line. It was so close she could taste it. Her body was full of nerves feeling like she'd accomplished the one thing that many other women could only imagine.

"What about tonight? I don't see any reason to wait any longer," he replied, rubbing the back of her hand.

"It's too late, silly, but what about first thing in the morning?" She smiled.

"Sounds great. So what about tonight?" He licked his lips and gently rubbed the hairs on his chin.

She knew exactly what he meant. She got up from her chair and he stood up as soon as she reached his side of the table. Getting so close that he could feel her breath on his neck she whispered, "Oh tonight, you let me take care of that." She turned and began to walk away. Kemp followed her, watching her leave before catching up. He briefly shook his head and smiled in anticipation of their evening and spending the rest of his life with his trophy wife.

While the union started off resembling something out of a fairy tale it didn't take long before things started to fray. Diamond's ulterior motives came to surface as soon as she had a pawn to play in her little game. Her previous relationship had molded her into a woman who refused to be used. Davey, her ex, swept her off of her feet by showering her with lavish gifts and tons of attention. Being adopted and, at that point, fatherless, it was easy to convince her that he was the man of her dreams. She'd do anything and everything for him hoping that her loyalty would make their love stand the test of time. Throughout their relationship she accepted things that most would frown upon. Despite being exploited, cheated on, and lied to she couldn't see her life without him. It wasn't until she went to prison for him and he hadn't even bothered to pick up the phone that enough was enough.

When she met Kemp, love was the furthest thing from her mind. His name rang dollars and, for her, that was the key ingredient to her success. In order to take all of his money she knew he'd have to be six feet under. She thought no way would he let her walk away from him rich. Knowing Kemp, he would leave her penniless; that was, unless she caught him red-handed in an affair.

Her childhood best friend, Mica, had recently come back into her life after five years of being separated. Mica, the sister of Diamond's first love, Johnny, had written her off as a friend. At the time, Johnny was serving a prison sentence for murdering their abusive father. Diamond had always pushed him to stand up for himself and protect his sister but she could have never known he would murder him. Mica blamed Diamond for Johnny's actions and after her mother moved to another section of the city they lost touch. Just like Diamond and many other females, Mica hadn't been able to resist Kemp's charm or bankroll either. Diamond wasn't sure when or how she'd get the opportunity to execute her plan but luckily for her they fell right in line. Kemp hadn't expected Diamond home and after Mica stopped by unexpectedly Kemp and Mica engaged in the ultimate betrayal. Enter Diamond, "the diva with a plan."

She could hear the moaning loudly through the halls, an instant indication that there was either a porno being watched, or another woman in her bed. Seeing how Mica's car was parked outside and her purse was on the table downstairs she had already put two and two together. Her footsteps couldn't be heard over their loud lovemaking, and not even the door opening interrupted them. She stood there in the dark hallway, watching, figuring she might as well let them finish before she let her presence be known. At least then it would all be worth it and they'd get some sort of enjoyment out of it all.

As Kemp lay flat on his back, his arms tightly gripped Mica's waist. She ground into him and let out moans each time the strokes hit her spot. The flickering of the candlelight bounced off of her body, making it radiant. Even the beads of sweat that formed on her back were evident. She continued to ride him jockey style and soon he was yelling her name and palming her ass until he had expelled every drop of his love inside of her.

She slowed her pace, and after stopping, Diamond, knew that it was her cue. She raised her gun and aimed it in their direction. She released the safety, which quickly gained their attention. Mica jumped off of him and began backing up to the top of the bed, covering her naked body with the sheets. Kemp sat up in shock and spoke, immediately trying to calm Diamond down.

In her mind she said, *Showtime. Let's get this over with so I can head straight to the bank.* But, just like an Academy Award–nominated actress, she turned on the waterworks, allowing the tears to fall from her face.

"Baby, it's not what you think." He spat the same bullshit line that every man speaks when they are caught.

What the fuck does he think? I'm blind? she thought. "What kind of asshole do you think that I am?" She screamed, "Did you actually think you could get away with this?"

"I'm so sorry you had to see this. I never wanted you to find out this way!" Mica cried, as tears began pouring out of her eyes. "I didn't want to hurt you."

"You didn't want to hurt me? That's bullshit! Fucking my man is definitely not the way to avoid it. I trusted you and this is what I get?" She pointed the gun again.

"Please, Diamond. Don't do this. This is not the way to handle this," Kemp continued to try his hand.

"Fuck you! You don't have the right to tell me what to do and what not to do. I'm running this shit! Do you see this gun? Remember this sight 'cause this is the last thing that you are going to see. I hope the pussy was worth it!" She cocked the gun and began shooting, releasing five shots. Blood sprayed all across the room, streaking the walls with a red texture.

It seemed to Diamond that every decision she made from that moment on was a result of the murders. She had to always look over her shoulder to make sure that there wasn't anyone lurking, or that she didn't do anything to tip off the police to her crimes. It was always a struggle and life would only get harder from that point. Luckily for Diamond, Black, Kemp's best friend, had stepped up to the plate. After the murders, Diamond frantically ransacked the house to make the murders appear to be part of a robbery gone wrong. Not knowing that Black was sitting in his car outside the house, she left the house in a hurry to figure out what her next move would be. Since Black always wanted to be with Diamond, saving her was instinct for him. Yes, Kemp was his best friend, but after years of being his shadow he was ready to take his spot in the limelight. Diamond was grateful for his help with covering up her crime and finally she was able to give him what he wanted: a full-blown relationship and Kemp's spot as a boss.

Things for the couple were going great until a letter came stating that she hadn't been successful in murdering both Kemp and Mica. Shaken up by the news, Diamond and Black struggled to stay afloat with someone wreaking havoc on their lives. After months of torment they learned that the culprit was Mica and not Kemp as they had been led to believe. Diamond was relieved that Kemp, the ruthless kingpin, was buried where she'd left him. This sense of relief was short-lived as Mica fingered Black for the murder of Kemp and attempted murder of her. During his prison stay, Diamond gave birth to a baby girl alone and was later kidnapped and saw her life flashing in front of her eyes. This time, Tommy, one of Black's men, was her knight in shining armor. With Mica finally gone, Black was free, and he and Diamond began their life together as a married couple.

Diamond hadn't known a love like Black and after a while she didn't even feel bad about being with him. Throughout the years that would follow and after all of the attempts on her life she still felt like being with Black was all worth it. Most people would look at Diamond and say that she deserved everything that she got, but deep down she truly believed that her current life was a reward for all of the heartache she experienced growing up. Being adopted, lied to, betrayed by everyone she loved, she couldn't do anything but bask in the glamour that her current life now displayed. Looking back, she didn't regret any of it, and looking forward she could see things only going up, especially with Mica totally out of the picture. Where it all began no longer mattered because, for Diamond and Black, it was a fresh start and it felt so right. . . .

Chapter One

Feels So Right

September 2010

"I can't believe it's been two years already," Black said as he stood up, facing the many family members and friends who quietly sat at the surrounding tables that filled the first floor of the Park Avenue Banquet Hall. The room was darkened with a bright light shining directly on to Black and Diamond's table, which sat in the front of the large room. The hall was tastefully decorated with the same colors they took their nuptials in two years earlier: teal, black, and white. Centerpieces filled with flowers that floated in blue-tinted water with silicone ice cubes blended with the rest of the décor.

Some of the attendees looked on and smiled in happiness, while some displayed evident looks of envy, wishing they could be as successful as the two guests of honor. Diamond and Black were celebrating their second wedding anniversary as well as their recent departure from the drug business. As planned, they'd invested in enough legal business to move on from the dangerous world that almost ripped them to shreds. They'd survived his imprisonment, her affair with Money, her near-fatal accident, as well as the attempt on both of their lives. After all that they'd been through, their relationship had blossomed into something much greater than anyone could have ever expected. They were the epitome of true love and, in current times, true love wasn't easy to find. With his glass raised in the air, Black looked over to his right and smiled at Diamond as she sat in a daydream taking it all in.

"I want to make a toast to the woman who has made this life worth living. Looking back I would've never thought that I'd be where I am today. I have a beautiful wife and a daughter I adore. I truly have everything that a man could dream of." He smiled while holding his glass up, thinking back to the moment he'd first laid eyes on Diamond. That was also the moment he knew he had to make her his wife. Realizing that he was getting more sentimental than normal he picked his speech back up. "Now, I'm going to stop being so mushy up here so we can get this party started." He laughed as the guests joined him, raising their glasses and toasting them with the others seated at their tables.

After a few seconds of laughter, the DJ increased the volume on the music and gradually people began to get up from their seats and migrate to the dance floor. Black sat down next to Diamond and stared at her for a few moments before she leaned in and broke the silence.

"That was beautiful, Black." She smiled. Her body was completely filled with joy. She couldn't remember another time in her life where she'd been this happy.

"Well I meant every word. You know you mean the world to me," he admitted while rubbing his hand across her cheek.

"Can you believe what we've accomplished? I mean things could have been disastrous for us but look how things turned out."

"That's because it was meant to be." He leaned in and kissed her softly on the lips.

"Uhhh, ummm, sorry to break you two love-birds up but would you mind if I stole the man of the hour for a dance?" Trice said as she grabbed Black by the hand.

"Not at all, as long as you promise to return him safely," Diamond replied, motioning with her hand and giggling.

"Scout's honor." Trice laughed and tugged at Black to pull him from his seated position. Trice, the mother of Black's son, had become one of Diamond's best friends. A few years back Diamond would have been ready for a fight but Trice had since moved on and was happily married herself. For the sake of the children, they'd all maintained an alliance that closely resembled a family. As Diamond watched Black and Trice bopping on the floor Tommy slid into the barren chair next to her.

"I know Mrs. Diamond isn't being a wallflower at her own party now." He laughed.

"Not at all, I'm just taking it all in. Besides, you know I'm the truth on the dance floor. You know you don't want to see me get busy." She burst into laughter.

"That's a sight I wouldn't mind seeing." He shook his head as the literal thought of Diamond "getting busy" crossed his mind.

"You are crazy, Tommy," she said and playfully shoved him.

"I'm serious." He laughed as she bashfully turned away.

Tommy secretly had a soft spot for Diamond, but out of respect for Black kept it to minor flirting every now and then. Diamond knew that Tommy felt something for her but she always managed to convince herself that he was just being a clown. She also had a place in her heart for him due to the fact that he saved her life when Mica and Money conspired to kill her. But she wasn't about to make the mistake of sleeping with the best friend of husband number two. The reality of the situation was that she actually loved Black and her new life. At that point she truly believed that there was nothing that they couldn't overcome.

"So what's up with you and your girl Alyssa? I thought you'd be marrying her for sure by now." She changed the subject.

"Yeah, right." He burst into laughter and flagged her with his right hand. "You know damn well that girl ain't the marrying type."

"Hell, I thought that's the kind of woman you like, that's all I ever see you with." She laughed.

"That's because the woman of my dreams isn't available at the moment." He gave a devilish grin.

Black came over to the table and interrupted the conversation. Diamond, relieved, quickly stood from her chair and grabbed Black's arm as he led her out to the dance floor. Tommy sat in the chair, sipping his Hennessy and Coke. As Black spun Diamond around on the floor and a crowd formed a circle to cheer them on, Tommy stared at the couple, imagining standing in Black's spot. He'd already taken the reins running the drug business, but Diamond would be the icing on the cake. Tommy was confident that the time would come when she'd need him and he would patiently wait for that day. For him, that would be the ultimate accomplishment.

As the time neared 2:00 a.m. the crowd began to disperse, and some of their guests grabbed trash cans to assist with the cleanup. Black sat drinking the last few drops of his Grey Goose vodka while Diamond and a few of her friends walked into the bathroom. Kiki, noticeably absent, had decided against attending the event after an argument with Diamond days earlier. Usually, the two had been able to squash their squabbles but this argument had morphed into more of a dual. The two had never been so distant and angry at one another. Though Diamond wanted everyone to believe she didn't care, the separation had taken a toll on her. She'd lost the one person she had always been able to talk to. She was now forced to keep all of her concerns, wants, needs, and aspirations to herself. Their small circle of friends had been waiting all night for the perfect time to question Diamond about her missing BFF. Finally, as they all headed into the ladies' room, they would get the chance that they'd been waiting for.

Diamond stood in front of the mirror re-touching her makeup and making sure her hair was perfect. The group of woman stood at different spots, all with the same question lingering in their minds. Diamond was always pretty quiet when it came to her personal business and not one of them was sure what they could ask without pissing her off. But, as they stood around the room appearing as if they had huge question marks over their heads, it was pretty evident that something was on their minds. Diamond realized that they were all just a bit too quiet and decided to break the silence to see what the hell was going on. Though she knew that most people didn't know how to approach her, she still believed that she was one of the easiest people to talk to.

"If someone wants to ask me a question, just do it. Standing there staring at each other won't get the answer that you are looking for." She paused to pucker her lips and apply her lip gloss. "I know it's about Kiki so what is it that you all want to know?"

All of the women appeared shocked and shook their heads as if they weren't concerned. Jasmine, the older of the bunch, stepped up and walked closer to where Diamond was standing. If there was one of them bold enough to go toe to toe with Diamond, it was Jasmine. The other three—Sydney, Palace, and Octavia—weren't as outspoken.

"Well yes, we do have a question. Kiki is supposed to be your best friend right? So, we really can't understand what could have been so important that she would miss your anniversary celebration."

Diamond shook her head briefly before grabbing a paper towel to dab off some of the excess gloss. "Jasmine, I think you just answered your own question with that statement, 'supposed to be.' Obviously she isn't, if she would miss one of the most important days of my life. Now, I don't cry over spilled milk because, honestly, she'll need me long before I need her. It's just sad that she would let a minor disagreement ruin our friendship after being my friend for so long. That makes me believe she was never really my friend to begin with." Diamond was now using her comb to tame the fly-aways in her hair.

The group of girls remained quiet, not wanting to press the issue any further. It was clearly a sore subject and rather than causing Diamond to feel as if she was being attacked, each of them believed it would be best to just drop it for the moment, knowing that it would all come up again in the future.

Jasmine, just as quickly as she asked the "Kiki" question, changed the subject. "Well, now that that's settled, what I really wanna know is where the hell the after-party is going down because I'm still fired up. I'm not ready to call it night just yet. And besides, I need to find a nice piece of meat to go home with if you know what I mean." She giggled while swirling her hips.

"I know that's right," Palace, who was also Jasmine's sister, agreed and slapped Jasmine a high five.

"I don't know but I'm sure Black isn't ready to go in either, so follow us and we can make sure wherever we decide to go everyone makes it into the VIP section," Diamond said as she returned all of her beauty tools to her bag and headed toward the door.

The group followed her as she walked through the ballroom and out of the front door, where Black and all of the other partygoers were standing. Luxury cars lined every edge of the street and they were so amped you could hear their chatter around the corner. Diamond loved seeing her man happy and it was at that moment she realized that they did the right thing by leaving the drug game. Her eyes were locked on Black as she switched as hard as she could and walked in his direction.

Once he noticed her, he rubbed the hairs on his chin and smiled. He had every intention of bending her over and waxing her ass all over their home that evening. His dick was getting hard from just the thought and he quickly adjusted his pants, hoping that no one noticed his quickly growing bulge.

"So where are we headed, babe?" she said, standing so close to him he could feel her breath tickling his skin. The sweet scent of her Juicy Couture Viva La Juicy perfume was flowing freely up his nostrils. "The girls were hoping we could swing by Vault since they are open until three-thirty. I know I'm not ready to call it a night so I was hoping that you weren't either." She smiled as he caressed her arm softly with his hand.

He was silent for a few seconds as his mind was totally consumed with how much he loved her. He'd never met a woman whom he would die for, literally. There was no limit to the things that he would do for her and he was positive that she felt the same way. "That's cool with me if that's what you wanna do," he finally replied.

"That's not *all* I wanna do, just what I wanna do at the moment." She giggled and playfully tugged at the bottom of her dress.

"Is that right?" he asked, adjusting his pants once again to hide his protruding manhood.

She laughed as she looked down at his crotch and back at his face. "Well let's go, before we end up ass naked in the back of this car."

"Yeah, we better." He smiled as he stood up off of his car. "Yo, Tommy, let's roll out, man. The ladies wanna hit Vault before we take it down."

Tommy nodded and obediently walked over to his car and ordered everyone else in their crew to do the same. Just like a funeral procession they all drove off one by one with Center City their destination.

Diamond sat in the passenger seat comfortably as they made their way through the city. Every so often she'd glance over at Black and smile. If there was anyone on this earth that she loved more than her baby girl, Dior, it was Black. Visions of their past flashed before her eyes. She felt blessed to be where she was at that moment, especially after all of the wrong that she had done to get there. If you would have asked her three years ago where she thought she'd be today she would've most likely shrugged her shoulders and said she didn't know, but if you asked her this day where she would be in three more years she would say happily ever after with Black.

Unfortunately, when you were on top there was always someone at the bottom clawing at your cuffs to pull you back down. With a jagged past and more enemies than they could keep up with, there could be someone lurking behind every corner, waiting for that brief second when they'd let their guard down. Diamond knew that they still had a lot more to do before "officially" being done with the drug life, but she wanted to enjoy this bliss as long as she possibly could.

Chapter Two

Brass Knuckles

Two men occupied a small eight-by-twelve concrete cell. Photos of hip hop video vixens and scantly clad female emcees covered the walls, with small pieces of tape holding them in place at each corner. One of the men was sprawled out on a metal-framed twin bed with a thin polyester mattress so hard it almost resembled the metal frame that lay beneath it. The man—dark skinned, weighing 230 pounds, all muscle, and standing six foot three inches tall—was resting his left hand behind his head and on top of the pillow. In his right hand, a book, *Strength to Love* by Martin Luther King Jr., had his full attention. One quote rang true: "All progress is precarious, and the solution of one problem brings us face to face with another problem." As he dragged his eyes across the pages of this 1963 release, he could only compare the statements to his own experiences. For him, every moment in his life was precarious and even the most detailed plan could crumble at any given moment, which was why he always prepared a plan B in the event that things went horribly wrong.

The second man, a mix of Puerto Rican and African American, almost resembling his cellmate in height and weight, was sitting up on the edge of his neatly made bed, with a black-and-white composition book in his right hand and a pencil in the other. On the pages were handwritten notes. The meaning of the notes was only understood by the two men who'd shared living quarters for the past two years.

"Yo, why are you always reading, man? Hell, at least read some shit that's interesting," Reed blurted out, breaking the eerie silence that had filled the room for the past hour.

"'Cause it ain't shit else to do. Might as well learn some shit while I'm still on this earth," Johnny replied, still keeping his eyes on the book.

"Aww, man, it's plenty to do like going over this plan, my nigga. I'm trying to make sure this shit is airtight. I don't want to end up back in here rooming wit' your ass." He laughed.

"Right now ain't the time for that shit. You see niggas walking up and down the block don't you? If you don't keep that shit on the low you'll definitely end up back in here. I'm going to die in here so I ain't got shit to lose. You on the other hand are just weeks away from freedom so keep that in mind."

Reed shook his head and closed the notebook before stuffing it under his pillow. He thought about how close he was to freedom and compared it to the life he'd lived for the past two years. Before he was booked his life was as close to perfect as a life could get. He was well known in the streets and had a team who ruled the drug game in Philadelphia, New Jersey, and Delaware also known as the tri-state area. Now, his wife was out there fending for herself after his team dispersed to different sets. Without a leader, the empire that he'd built from the ground up quickly crumbled to bits and pieces. Luckily, he had a few loyal men who had maintained his relationships with his suppliers and kept a steady flow of narcotics and cash flowing while he was away. He was anxious to get back on top and with Johnny's help he was going to do just that.

Thinking back, he reminisced about the good times. Hanging out partying, spending money, and sexing beautiful and exotic women left and right. Now, a normal day consisted of washing dishes, playing basketball, working out in the yard, and hanging out in the cell with Johnny. He had no privacy—he couldn't even shit in peace. Even worse than boredom and the lack of serenity, he was being tested on a daily basis by other inmates who thought he was weak, or just felt like he had something that they wanted. Unfortunately for them he proved that he was far from weak each time he laid them out flat on their asses.

Unlike Johnny, Reed had a lot to live for; his wife, Raquel, and his five-year-old princess, Alyia, were all the inspiration he needed to keep going every day. A photo and vivid flashes of memories were all that kept him sane and it was them who were also what kept him from copping a murder charge behind bars. As the day neared when he could walk out of the hellhole that he'd been forced to call home and return to Philly to get things back on track, his anxiety became more evident.

His plan went beyond the tasks that Johnny wanted him to complete. He knew that he had to have another plan since Johnny's motives were that of pure revenge. Making decisions on that alone could land you six feet under, or in prison for the rest of your life. Reed was determined to stay out of prison by any means necessary. He refused to be one of those statistics that you see on TV. Living with Johnny had taught him a lot. It showed him just how little a nigga with a grudge cared about the things he stood to lose. In his mind, he figured that it was a lonely place—one that he never wanted to take a trip to.

After a few minutes of dullness, Reed retrieved the notebook from under his pillow again but decided to read it silently rather than asking Johnny about it. He felt like a student preparing for a final exam or turning in a term paper. He wanted to be certain that he'd crossed every "t" and dotted every "i." As he read the codes, which were scribbled on the pages, the symbol that represented the name of his main target stood out: *Diamond.* He wondered how a woman with a name so beautiful could wreak so much havoc on a man's life that he'd want to destroy everything that she loved. He hadn't seen a photo of her just yet, but by the way that Johnny described her he could imagine her without even one glance.

"So can I ask you a question, man?" Reed once again broke the silence and interrupted Johnny's concentration on the book that he was reading.

Closing the book and sitting up on the edge of the bed, Johnny asked, "What, man? It's obvious that you aren't going to let me finish my daily reading so go ahead and ask. This shit better be good, too, for you to interrupt me twice while I'm gaining some knowledge," he said, annoyed.

"Were you ever in love with this girl? I'm just curious because there has to be some sort of feelings in order to hate a person so much." Reed could tell by the look on Johnny's face that he was annoying him but he didn't care; he just wanted to learn as much about her as he could.

"Yeah, I loved her. She was my first love, hell my only love. Shit she was my girlfriend when I got arrested. Shit, I thought we would have been together forever. I thought she would stay down for me while I was locked away but it wasn't until my letters went unanswered that I realized how far from reality that actually was." He paused and shook his head. "My sister was my life and I felt like the biggest asshole on the planet when she told me how different Diamond had turned out to be. She looked me in the eye and said the girl I once knew and loved was long gone and would never return."

"So, I'm still a little confused, because I still don't get how a teenage love lost could cause so much anger and rage," Reed replied honestly.

"Man, this ain't got shit to do with teenage love. This bitch took away the one person who always had my back. My sister is dead because of her and now my mother has lost both of her children. I'm gonna die in here, man. If it's the last thing I do before I take my final breath that bitch is gonna pay for what she's done."

Reed looked at him still longing for more information. He wanted to know what role she played in the death of his sister. He decided not to ask him any more questions at that moment because he could tell Johnny was on the verge of breaking down. Though all of his siblings were still living he could feel his pain. He knew, if put in the same situation, he would feel the exact same way.

Johnny looked over at Reed and let out a laugh. The laugh was intended to downplay the seriousness of the conversation with the hopes that he wouldn't ask him any more questions. "Is that sufficient enough for you?" Johnny blurted out.

Laughing, Reed replied, "Yeah, man, for now, but we still got a lot more to talk about, especially if you want me to risk my life to settle a score that isn't even mine to begin with."

"That's fair enough, and I promise you will know everything there is to know about me, my past, and little Miss Diamond before your departure from Hotel Hell," he said and extended his hand to shake on it.

Reed obliged and with that he closed the composition book once again and placed it back underneath the pillow for safekeeping. He wasn't 100 percent satisfied with the information that he was given, but he knew that it made no sense to keep pressing a man who obviously had something to hide. "It's cool, man, I'll drop it for now, but we only have a few weeks to get things straight. Just keep in mind, I don't like going into any situation blind, so I need any and all information no matter how small or unimportant it may seem to you. In order for me to do my job right you have to supply me with the proper tools. You know what I'm saying?"

"I know exactly what you're saying and I got it. I hear your concerns loud and clear," Johnny replied. With just a short time left before Reed would be released, Johnny knew he had a limited amount of time to give him a suitable explanation for taking a life. Saying that she was the reason Mica was dead wasn't the same as her being the one who murdered her. Death by association clearly wasn't enough for Reed, and Johnny had to cleverly lay out the clues without allowing Reed a moment to feel sorry for Diamond and change his mind. This was Johnny's last chance since his health was quickly deteriorating and he never knew which day would ultimately be his last.

Reed lay across his bed and drifted off in deep thought, awake but with closed eyes. Quietly, he was thinking more about his own plan than Johnny's. He knew that he needed to go through with it all in order to get the money that he needed to purchase the weight necessary for his own survival. As many times as he tried, he couldn't figure out how to get the money without extortion or murder. Though he didn't *know* Diamond, he did know his own wife and daughter, and because of that he couldn't get completely comfortable with taking a mother away from her child, or vice versa. The way that he saw it, Johnny would be dying soon anyway and as far as he knew, he had no drug or gang ties to make any noise out on the streets. So, the key would be finding a way to make Johnny believe that the job was done just until he could take the money he needed and run. He also contemplated what he'd do if Johnny was actually setting him up to take a fall or, even worse, be murdered. He felt confident that his street smarts would assist him if he had to fight tooth and nail for his own life. However, there was always a chance that he could be blindsided and he had to expect the unexpected.

Johnny sat on the other side of the room with similar thoughts. Something in his heart told him that Reed would try to screw him if he got the chance, and he had just the thing for him in the event that things went totally left. As much as he didn't want to believe that Reed's betrayal was a possibility he had to prepare himself for the worst. His backup plan would allow him to deal with Diamond and Reed if necessary. In the past two years, the pair had become close friends, or so they liked to think. They'd even fought numerous bloody battles in the yard when fellow inmates attacked without warning. They'd always looked out for one another, but Johnny's time in the penitentiary had shown him how important it was to keep your friends closer than your enemies, since they were the ones to drive the dagger into your back as soon as you were caught slipping. That one lesson was the realest lesson he'd learned and not one book in any library could have taught him that. Learning how to grow eyes in the back and both sides of your head was *priceless*.

Soon, you could hear the correction officer's signal and then the lights went out. After a few minutes of chatter among the inmates, a few of them spewing obscenities at the guards and other inmates, the block was filled with silence. Johnny and Reed relaxed in their own private darkness until they drifted off to sleep, both men armed with a handy pair of mental brass knuckles in case there ever came a time when a secret weapon was needed, both prepared to go to war at the drop of a dime.

Chapter Three

Frenemies

"All I'm saying is she wouldn't have shit if it weren't for me. I mean seriously, I went out of my way to make sure she lived more than comfortably. Shit, she was living in a small-ass apartment, going from hustla to hustla trying to score a kingpin when all she scored were some wet panties and a cold bed. If I wanted to be a real bitch, I could shut that fucking club down," Diamond said with an abundance of attitude, as she sat and ate dinner with Black at their tulip tree–wood dining room table.

"I don't get women, man, y'all two were the best of friends and now you're ready to shut her whole life down because of some he said, she said shit? Diamond, that's just crazy and I'm sorry, babe, I love you more than life itself but I have to disagree with your actions on this one." He shook his head before taking a bite of his slice of supreme Pizza Hut pizza.

"So my husband is just going to take another bitch's side over mine?" She raised her voice as she visibly became more annoyed. Both of her eyebrows were raised and her lips were twisted.

"I didn't say I was taking her side, Diamond, I just said you're being a bit childish. I don't understand why you two can't just have an adult conversation and straighten this shit out," Black replied before taking a swig of his Pepsi soda. "You can sit and twist your face, pout and all that shit, Diamond, but you can't be right all the time. If you were ever really friends you would be able to squash it."

"First of all, I'm not pouting, and can we just change the subject? Because I feel myself getting angry and I'd hate to report to my anger management counselor that I murdered my *second* husband," she said, rolling her eyes.

"Oh, so you're gonna murder me, huh?" Black asked before wiping the excess pizza crumbs from his mouth with his napkin.

Diamond sat mum as he placed the napkin down and slid his chair out from under the table. With seriousness written all across his face, he walked behind Diamond's chair and placed both of his large hands around her neck. "I didn't hear a response. You plan on murdering me?" He tightened his grip.

She pushed his hands off of her neck and quickly rose from her seat, turning around to face him. "I will if I have to," she replied.

Without speaking Black pushed the chair that sat in between them to the floor, and threw Diamond's plate of uneaten pizza to the floor, causing the glass to crack into bits and pieces all over the area rug. He stood face to face with her for a few moments, staring her in the eye as she tried her hardest not to blink. Unexpectedly, he grabbed both of her ass cheeks and picked her up on to the table, and with a quick hand motion his hands went under her dress and ripped her thong off of her. He threw them to the floor and grabbed her by the neck.

"Let me hear you say that again," he breathed into her ear while dropping his lounge pants to the floor and thrusting his rock-hard dick inside of her moist pussy, which welcomed him with opened lips.

"Ummm, damn baby," she moaned while grabbing hold of the tablecloth that lay beneath her.

Black continued to fuck her, using every muscle in his legs to push all ten inches of his thick meat inside of her. "You like that shit?" he asked while lightly squeezing her neck with one hand and using the other to pull her closer to him for a deeper penetration.

"I like it," she whispered.

"I can't hear you. What did you say?" he yelled while pumping harder and harder. You could hear his thighs slapping up against the table echoing through the house. Her pussy juices were pouring out of her and forming a small puddle underneath her. She loved when he was forceful—it turned her on.

"I like it," she said one octave louder than she had previously.

Black, still not satisfied with that answer, began to fuck her faster and harder. Every time he'd pull himself out of her, he'd leave just the head in, bend his knees and stand back up with force, almost lifting her ass one inch off of the table. "You said you like it, is that it? You only *like* this dick huh?" His deep voice was rumbling through the house.

"Ohhhh shit, Black, I'm about to cum. I'm gonna cum all over this fucking dick," she yelled as her legs wrapped tightly around his waist, grinding the tip of his stiff dick right into her G-spot and causing her body to shake uncontrollably, releasing her cum all over the entire shaft.

"Damn, baby, this pussy is soaking wet," he whispered, feeling himself nearing an eruption.

Diamond used her hands to lift herself off of the table. With her legs still wrapped around his waist she forced her pussy onto his dick continuously, while moving her hips in a circular motion.

"Baby, ooh shit, goddamn, baby, here it comes," he yelled as he released his cum inside of her for what felt like an eternity. His legs became weak and his arms could barley hold on to the table.

Diamond released him from her leg grip so he could sit down. Once he sat in the seat, both of them burst into laughter.

"We have to do that shit more often, damn!" he said aloud.

"Well now that we got that out the way, I guess I can take your advice and try to iron out this issue with Kiki," she spoke through twisted lips as she slid off of the table, trying to fix her ruffled clothing.

"That's my girl." Black smiled as he looked down at his dick, which was still rock hard. "Now let's take care of this before you go."

She smiled and walked over to him, bent over, and grabbed hold of his dick before getting in a squatting position and wrapping her thick lips around it. From behind, you could see her voluptuous frame and well-rounded ass cheeks moving up and down. Her sculpted calf muscles were glistening from the beads of sweat forming all over her body. She was working overtime, using every trick up her sleeve to satisfy her man.

Feeling himself nearing an orgasm he firmly gripped the arms of the chair with both hands and slightly lifted his butt off of the chair to push his dick deeper down her throat. A few moments later he was in pure heaven as he released every drop that he had left into her mouth. Without hesitation, she quickly swallowed his juices, not allowing any of it to slip from the sides of her mouth. His body was still shaking seconds later when she stood over him and stared him in the face.

"Are you okay?" she asked with a giggle, while she attempted to fix her disheveled clothing.

"I'm good, as a matter of fact I'm greeee-aaaatttt," he jokingly replied, imitating the voice of Tony the Frosted Flakes tiger.

The two laughed in sync before Diamond headed upstairs to shower. Her intention for the following day was to contact Kiki and see how they could get past this hurdle that they were experiencing. Black was right: at some point one of them needed to be mature, and if Kiki wasn't going to be the one to take the first step it wouldn't kill Diamond to do so.

The following day Diamond went about her normal routine, getting Dior off to daycare and doing her morning runs. She knew Kiki was usually working by twelve noon so she figured that would be the perfect time to go and talk with her, assuming that she was there alone.

Diamond arrived to find only Kiki's car in the parking lot of the club. Diamond took a deep breath before heading to the entrance to ring the bell. A few moments later she could hear the sound of Kiki's stilettos nearing the door.

Kiki could see that it was Diamond on the camera and was at first hesitant before opening it. She wasn't in the mood for a physical confrontation and she'd known Diamond long enough to know how she got down. But, she knew that it was probably wise to just get the conversation over with, as it was long overdue. The two women definitely had some things to hash out so she sincerely hoped that they could do so like mature adults.

"Long time no see. You're not hiding a gun behind your back are you?" Kiki asked jokingly, attempting to break the thick ice.

"Naw, if I had a gun I certainly wouldn't hide it." Diamond laughed.

"Come on in. I just got here." Kiki waved with her hands.

Diamond entered the building and made her way through the corridor that led to the office.

She stepped inside after noticing the rest of the club was darkened besides that small office. She helped herself to a seat on the plush leather sofa, which sat in one corner of the room. She patiently waited with her legs crossed as Kiki made her way into the room.

"So what's been up, Ms. Kiki? I figured it was time that we talked," Diamond blurted.

"Same ol', just trying to stay afloat, and yes, it was definitely time that we talked. I mean I can't believe that we went this long without having a conversation." She sat down on the edge of her desk.

"Well, Black insisted that I come straighten things out. I mean, honestly, I can't even remember why we weren't speaking," Diamond replied.

"Well my issue with you started after the whole murder plot against you. It really hurt me when you accused me of knowing something about it. Yes, I was sleeping with JB but he never let me know about a plot to set you up. He used me the same way he used you and Black. I would never conspire with Mica to have you murdered and if I had known I most certainly would have told you. I thought that our friendship was stronger than that. I just couldn't get past that, Diamond, that shit hurt like hell," she said in a low tone.

"I apologized about that, Kiki. I mean you have to understand what I was going through. I didn't know who I could trust. I felt like everybody was out to get me. I can't take back the past but I am sorry that I hurt you; that was never my intention. That was the worst time of my life, one of the lowest points. I thought that we had worked through that, Kiki." She sat there confused.

"I thought we did, Diamond, but when your new circle of friends came in the picture I felt the distance between us. Everything changed. You never talked to me about anything anymore. It was like I always had to hear shit from other people. You were shutting me out."

"And it wasn't intentionally. I was just so unsure of everything. My world had been turned upside down."

"I know that, Diamond, I was a part of your life. Did you ever stop to think how my life has changed? Did you ever think of how it all affected me?"

Diamond sat silent, pondering the questions that Kiki posed. She was absolutely right; she'd never thought about how Kiki felt. When things came crashing down the only people she thought about were herself, Dior, and Black. Sadly, Kiki never crossed her mind. Maybe it was a bit selfish, and that was something that she'd always been told about herself. It was something that she worked to change, but she wasn't perfect, so there would be times that slipped through the cracks.

"You're right, Kiki, I didn't think about you and I'm sorry. I love you, Kiki, you are the closet thing to a sister that I have. I never wanted to shut you out and I can swear on a stack of Bibles. I need you back in my life. I feel like there's a piece of me missing without you," she said honestly.

Kiki sat relieved. She was hoping that things would turn out this way. It made her feel like a huge weight had been lifted off of her shoulders now that she'd been able to get Diamond to see that she was wrong. Instead of responding with words Kiki eased off of the desk and walked over to hug Diamond. As Diamond stood to hug her, both of them held in tears. Regardless of the outer appearances the two had portrayed during their time apart, they loved each other and both women were silently thanking Black for nudging Diamond to move on from the past.

"Now, when can I see my goddaughter? I know she is so big now!" Kiki laughed.

"You can see her whenever you want!" She smiled.

The two women sat and caught each other up on life and what they'd missed. Within minutes it was as if they'd never been separated to begin with. The two frenemies were back to being friends.

Chapter Four

Back Against the Wall

Reed stood at the exit of the prison, waiting for the gates to open to let him out on to the street. So many thoughts were running through his head and not even the anticipation of seeing his family could steady it. He wanted to enjoy his freedom but he knew that it wouldn't immediately be something to celebrate. He looked back over his shoulder one last time before taking the steps through the large metal gate to find his right-hand man, Romeo, waiting patiently, posted up against a brand-new Mercedes-Benz CL-Class, all black with shiny rims. Though he expected his wife to be there to pick him up he was happy to see Romeo. It instantly bought back memories of better days and moneymaking escapades. He smiled as he put some pep in his step in order to reach his chariot in record time.

"Daaaaaaamnnnnnnnn, I see life is treating you well. Nigga, this ride is the shit. Can't wait to get back up, man." He reached out to Romeo to engage in their signature handshake and hug. They patted each other on the back a few times before finally separating.

Romeo looked at him with a huge grin before replying, "You like this shit, man?"

"Like? Nigga I *love* this shit, man. You can't get a better Benz than this. This shit is top of the line."

"Well it's yours, man," Romeo said before pulling a set of keys from his pocket and dangling them in the air in front of his face.

"You bullshittin' me?" he asked with a laugh.

"Have I ever bullshitted you, man?" He paused, waiting for an answer, knowing he wouldn't give him one. "Now take these keys, hop in, and let's get the fuck outta here. I got warrants and shit. I can't be out here too long if you know what I mean." He laughed and dropped the keys in the palm of Reed's hand.

Reed opened the door and threw his bag of belongings in the back seat. He couldn't wait to feel the gas pedal under his foot and watch the sight of the prison slowly disappearing from his rearview mirror.

"How does it feel, man? I know it's been a long time coming. I know how that shit felt when I was locked up and, shit, that was only for six months! Nigga, I would lose my damn mind if I had to be caged up like that for two years." He laughed.

"Shit, man, all I could think about was coming home. The past few weeks couldn't come fast enough for me. Those days felt like months. I can't wait to get home to my wife, man. I told her not to visit so she wouldn't have to see me caged in, but I regretted that shit because I missed her like crazy." He shook his head in excitement.

"I wanna talk to you about her, man. Shit's done changed since you've been away." Romeo's tone went from happiness to seriousness in a matter of seconds.

"What the fuck you mean shit's changed? And don't beat around the bush; just give that shit to me raw!" His smile had diminished and turned to a frown.

"Yo, about a year into your bid she started fucking with the young gun Brook. She put your crib up for sale and moved to Jersey, man. I took the money down to the Realtor to buy that shit so you wouldn't lose it."

Rage instantly flowed through Reed's veins. To avoid causing an accident, he slammed on the

brakes, as he needed a few minutes to process
what Romeo had just said. Romeo sat quiet
waiting for Reed to say something but his eyes
were looking down at the floor as both of his
hands were firmly gripping the steering wheel.
He couldn't even think straight. He'd never
wanted to kill someone as much as he did at that
moment. He was certain if he saw Brook it would
take at least ten men to keep his hands from
choking him to death.

Just the thought of another man having sex
with his wife was almost enough to make him
vomit. The woman he'd devoted everything to
for the majority of his adult life had betrayed
him in the worst way possible. *How could she?*
he thought. If it weren't for him she'd still be
a ghetto project bitch living off government
assistance. She would have never had the pleasure of riding around in luxury cars or wearing
jewelry that cost more than people's homes.
His friends had clowned him for marrying her
because they were certain that she poked holes
in the condoms to ensure her ticket out of the
hood. Regardless of how they tried to influence
him to leave her ass stranded at the altar, he
couldn't live comfortably knowing that he'd left
the mother of his child to struggle when he lived
in a $300,000 house on the hill.

"Do you know where they stay at?" Reed asked through clinched teeth.

"Naw, not the exact address; I know the area, but I can find out for you. I got some niggas who owe me a few favors."

"And, what about Alyia? Does this bitch have my baby girl shacking up with some random wannabe thug?"

"Naw, she's with her mother. I take money over there every month, man, just like I promised I would. I would've wrote you while you were gone to update you but I didn't want you to get all angry and shit and fuck up your probation. I made sure your baby girl was good but Raquel, I haven't given her a dime since she did that slimy shit, man."

"Does she know that I was coming home?"

"I'm sure she does, you know how fast word gets around in the streets. I haven't seen her in the hood but that don't mean shit. I haven't seen that nigga Brook either but he certainly ain't untouchable."

Romeo hated to be the bearer of bad news. Even though he'd prepared himself to spill the beans, he didn't expect to see the hurt in Reed's eyes. He'd known him since grade school so he could see right through his anger. "I'm sorry, Reed, real talk. I wish this shit was all a joke and your homecoming could've been a bit more welcoming. I hate to see you hurting."

"It ain't your fault that I married a conniving bitch, and eventually I'm gonna deal with her. I just need to handle some other shit first." He twisted the key in the ignition and began the drive toward his home. He was happy that he had at least one true friend in the world to make sure that he could live comfortably once he was released. "Since I still have a home to go to, let's be on our way. I hope you got some alcohol and some bitches lined up for me, too. I ain't smelled pussy in two years. I'm wayyyyyyy overdue." He laughed, attempting to hide how angry and hurt he actually was.

"You know I got you covered; it wouldn't be me if I didn't." He joined in laughter with Reed.

The remainder of the ride went pretty silent besides the few times they passed a group of people they knew on the streets. Just like a celebrity or a rapper, Reed still got the same respect that he did prior to his arrest. After each wave or yell he felt good for a brief moment until the realization of his broken home popped up in his mind. After finally reaching the cul-de-sac that led to his home, his nerves began to go wild. Most likely the thought of life being totally different shook him up a bit. When they arrived at his driveway they noticed a white Porsche Cayman S parked behind Romeo's Range Rover. Romeo used his arm to signal Reed to slow down and approach the driveway cautiously.

"Yo, I think that's Raquel's car parked right there. What the fuck is she doing here?" Romeo asked, annoyed by the sight of the gold digger who he truly believed was the biggest mistake in Reed's life.

"Word? This bitch has balls the size of King Kong to roll up here after the shit you just told me." He stopped just short of the driveway and, without turning the engine off, he swung the door open with force and jumped out of the car.

Raquel opened her car door and swung her legs around, planting her Jimmy Choos on the ground before standing. She was dressed in a black jumpsuit that hugged her curves and created a camel-toe effect in her crotch, which under different circumstances would normally turn Reed on. She looked like a runway model with her long hair flowing freely and blowing in the wind. With one hand, she removed her Luxuriator Style 23 shades from her eyes. She looked like a million bucks, literally, as the cost of the car and her attire would set a low-grade hustla way back trying to keep up. But as beautiful as she was, it wouldn't erase the fact that she'd hopped on the next dick smoking when the going got tough. That was an unforgivable offense that would be punishable by public stoning in other countries.

Reed began to walk toward her with Romeo following closely behind in the event that she had goons lurking in the background.

"So I see not much has changed since you went away. As usual you have an obedient guard dog by your side." She laughed.

Reed laughed to try to avoid lunging at her neck and slowly choking the life out of her. He remained as cool as he possibly could under the circumstances since he certainly didn't want to be hauled back to prison. "I can't believe that you have the audacity to show up here after you abandoned all of my property and our daughter for some punk-ass dealer who was practically a servant of mine for years," Reed replied, as he now stood about three feet away from her.

"That's funny that you can stand here with a straight face and say some shit like that. My shades cost more than half of what this house is worth. Obviously he's worth more than you ever were."

"Bitch, let me explain something to you real quick," he said as he pounded his left fist into his right hand as most men did when they were trying to get a point across. "I should've left your trifling ass in those filthy, pissy-ass projects. That shit could've saved me years of stress and aggravation."

"Well, you didn't, and if you regret it then that's just too damn bad. I didn't come here to engage in small talk and as much as I would just *love* to catch up on the past two years I have some official business to take care of." She reached into her car and retrieved a large manila envelope before holding it out in his direction.

"What the hell is this?" he asked, snatching the envelope from her hand.

"Open it and see," she snapped.

He opened the envelope to find divorce papers citing irreconcilable differences. Almost instantaneously he felt nothing but disgust and hatred for the woman he vowed to stick with for better or worse. He shook his head before being brutally honest about his feelings for her at that moment. "You know you are the most vindictive and trifling bitch I've ever laid eyes on. If you were a man you'd be snoring on the concrete right now after I'd knocked you the fuck out. I should break your fucking face to pieces to disfigure you just enough to knock you off of that high horse you're sitting on. You can take these damn divorce papers and shove them up your pretty little ass. I wish I would give you the pleasure of taking what's mine. Bitch, I don't owe you shit," he yelled with spit flying from his lips. His body was filled with so much rage that it was becoming more difficult by the second to contain it.

"Well I suggest you hire a good lawyer because I can't stay married to you another day. I have a man at home who provides more for me physically and emotionally than you're capable of."

"I couldn't care less about your suggestions, or anything that has to do with you for that matter. You can take your stuck-up, gold-digging ass back to your bitch-ass man and tell him I'll be seeing his ass around real soon," he yelled.

"Yeah, we'll see how much of bitch he is when you meet face to face." She laughed as she turned to walk back to her car. "I'll be seeing you soon, smooches," she said before puckering her lips into a kiss.

He stood there shaking his head in disbelief. He couldn't believe that this was the same woman he'd fallen in love with so many years ago. The ride-or-die-chick façade was proving to be faker than a thirty dollar bill. He turned to look at Romeo, who was shaking his head as well.

"Scandalous-ass bitch," Romeo yelled. He could feel Reed's pain as he, too, had been through many women in his day; you always had to get through a bunch of rocks before you found a diamond.

"What a homecoming, man." Reed laughed.

Romeo walked over to his car to remove it from the driveway to allow Reed to pull his car in. As Reed sat in his car he used the silence to reflect on the choices that he'd made in his life. He wondered if this was punishment for all of the wrong that he'd committed. Reed parked and exited his car.

Romeo rolled down his window. "I'm gonna come in with you to do a walk-through, then I have to go handle some shit."

"Cool, I have some shit to handle myself," Reed replied before walking over to the front door.

Romeo exited his car and walked behind Reed as he entered the house. Turning on the light Romeo took a quick surveillance.

"Home sweet home. I thought that I'd be opening my front door and having my baby girl running into my arms."

"I know, man." Romeo patted Reed on his shoulder. "Everything happens for a reason. I'm a strong believer of that shit. It's a good thing you saw that shit now, man. I'm gonna roll out now to make a few runs but I'm gonna swing back around eight, 'cause I got a lot of shit planned for you tonight."

"All right, I'll be ready for sure."

"And wipe that frown off your face; fuck her for real. It's plenty of bad bitches out here. Seriously," Romeo said before reaching out to shake Reed's hand. Reed walked Romeo to the door and slowly shut it behind him. "Home sweet fucking home," he said aloud as he shook his head in disbelief. He walked around the house, looking at the things that were the same as well as the things that were different. He was glad to be home but he was frustrated that things weren't going to be the way that he'd left them. Walking into his kitchen he remembered the mornings where his daughter would sit eating her breakfast and swinging her legs in her high chair. He pictured her little face and her smile. Even with her mother being the bitch she was, he could at least thank her for giving him the daughter he loved more than life itself.

He headed upstairs to the master bedroom and found a fresh pair of Prada sneakers with the matching leather belt, a black button up, and crisp dark blue Rock & Republic jeans. He smiled, knowing that Romeo was probably the only person on this earth who knew him better than or just as well as he knew himself. It was certainly going to feel good to rock designer threads instead of prison blues. He hurried to shower so he could get started on his stops to make it back in time to meet Romeo at eight. Though his day hadn't started out as well as he would have liked, he was going to make the best of whatever was thrown his way. The hot water, steam, and the smell of Zest body wash filled the bathroom with a relaxing aroma, just what he needed to prepare him for the night ahead.

Chapter Five

His Little Secret

"So, how are things with your new boo?" Diamond asked, playfully nudging Kiki on her shoulder.

"Who said he was my boo?" Kiki laughed.

"Well you said that you had a friend. I mean excuse me if I *thought* that was what you meant." She laughed as she shook her head.

"I'm joking, girl, yes, he is my boo and things are going great."

"I'm happy for you. I really hope things work out."

"Shit, me too. Lord knows I've had my fair share of assholes along the way." She took a sip of her juice.

"So how are you enjoying life away from the game?"

"It's nice to have the weight off of my shoulders but I miss the control. It's nothing like being the boss of an empire like that. That's a once-in-a-lifetime situation. Plus Black is only eighty percent out of the game. I still sit up at night waiting for him to come home. I always worry that some jealous-ass nigga is going to try to take him out as soon as his back is turned."

"I thought you were officially out."

"Yeah, I thought so too, but Black is still in the streets more than he's home. He claims that there are things that he has to wrap up and it's taking a lot longer than he expected. I think it's bullshit, he probably never had any intention of leaving the game in the first place."

Kiki sat shaking her head, clueless. Though she hadn't been around for a year, she'd heard through the grapevine that they were done. She wondered why he'd make promises and plans that he never intended to keep. She wasn't sure what to say to her friend, as it was obvious that there was trouble in paradise. She remembered being envious of their relationship. She remembered how much they were in love and how Black doted on her. If there was any couple that would last forever, it was them. For as long as she'd known Diamond she couldn't remember a time when she was happier than she was with Black. "But are things good between you two?" Kiki asked after a few seconds of silent thoughts.

"I mean things are okay, but not as good as I would like them to be," she admitted. If there was one thing that Diamond hated, it was to look like a failure. She would do anything in her power to avoid that.

"Aww, D, I am sorry things aren't turning out the way that you planned."

"Girl, don't be sorry, it ain't your fault." She flagged her, attempting to brush it off. "You know me though, I've got a strategy. I refuse to lose my man." She cracked a smile.

"Oh I know you always think on your feet. I'm just worried, D. I know how much you love him and how much you went through to keep him. I just hope that you are as important to him as he is to you."

"I don't doubt that, Kiki, not one bit. I just think that he has his priorities a little screwed up, but he'll get it together."

"Well, hate to cut you short, baby girl, but I have to go open the club. If you need to talk call me, okay?" she said before getting up and walking over to hug Diamond. After the two embraced, Diamond walked Kiki to the door. Just as she was leaving Black pulled up in the driveway. "Speak of the devil," she said with a big smile.

"What does that mean?" Black asked, rubbing his hands across his beard as he normally did when he was deep in thought.

"I was just chatting with the missus that's all." She turned to look at Diamond as she stood in the door. Black stared at Kiki without saying a word. Diamond stood at the door, looking on. Kiki put her sunglasses on her forehead and twisted her lips. "Don't get your boxers in a bunch, Black, I kept quiet."

He looked at her and then looked over at Diamond before turning his attention back to Kiki. "I knew you would, especially if you want to keep breathing," he responded through clinched teeth.

Kiki began to laugh before giving Diamond a final wave and walking toward her car. Black nodded and made his way to the door. He kissed Diamond before she spoke.

"What was all that about?"

"Oh, she was just thanking me for pushing you to contact her." He lied, knowing if she knew the truth he'd practically have to take a lie detector test to keep their relationship together. Deep down, he felt like the biggest asshole on the planet. He wasn't prepared to lose his family and he would do whatever it took to make sure of that. In his eyes, Diamond was still the woman he fell in love with and wanted to spend the rest of his life with.

After entering the house, Black made his way upstairs without saying much to Diamond. Their relationship had gradually been changing and she couldn't figure out why. As she watched him walk up the steps without any conversation she remained in the living room shaking her head. At first, she was going to let him have his space and get through whatever it was that he needed to do, but this had been dragged out long enough. She noticed Black sitting on the edge of the bed, finishing up a phone conversation when she walked in the room.

"What's going on with us, Black?" she said in a low tone.

Black turned around and shot her a look of seriousness. "What are you talking about, Diamond?"

"You know what I mean, Black. Three weeks ago we were fine, now it's like we barely talk. I'm trying to figure out what the issue is so that I can fix it."

"Diamond, you know what I'm trying to do and what's consuming my time. I'm just tired that's all. You're thinking too much and turning nothing into something. There isn't an issue to fix, okay? Nothing is wrong."

"Black, please don't shut me out," she pleaded with a single tear dropping from her right eye. She knew Black like the back of her hand and she knew that there was something wrong. She immediately thought back to the time she purposely stopped her birth control pills to get pregnant. During that time, he was still sleeping with Trice, his son's mom. She knew that he was sleeping around but she couldn't really prove it. She wasn't about to lie down without a fight so she devised a plan that got her the engagement ring and husband. Without Dior, Black might have strayed, but there was something about seeing his baby girl that made him a better man. He wanted to be the man his daughter could be proud of, not a man who would walk out and leave them to fend for themselves. Diamond stood there, lost, trying desperately to figure out what was bothering him.

Black looked over at her and noticed her tears. He hated to see her cry, especially when he was the one causing the pain. "Diamond, why are you crying? I just told you there wasn't anything wrong. I just have a lot on me right now that's all. I wish you would start taking my word instead of coming up with your own ideas."

Figuring that she'd never be able to get him to come clean, she shook her head and walked out of the room. She had a gut feeling that there was another woman and now she needed to devise another plan to regain his attention. Over the years she'd learned how to use what she had to get whatever it was that she wanted, and this time wasn't any different.

Confident that she was out of ear's reach, Black pressed redial on his phone. "Sorry I hung up on you but she was coming in," Black whispered into the phone while walking to close the bedroom door.

"Yeah, I figured that," the female on the other end responded. "So when can I see you? I miss you like crazy. It's killing me."

"Tomorrow for sure. I have some shit to handle early in the day but I can swing by after five if that's cool."

"Of course. At this point I will take what I can get. I know you have to split your time and I'm okay with that, as long as I get some of your time."

Black laughed. "Well I will see you tomorrow. I'm about to take a quick nap before I head back out."

"Okay, well, sleep well."

"I will," he said before ending the call.

Diamond quietly stood outside of the door, devastated. The conversation confirmed her suspicions. She wanted to burst into the room and let him know that he was caught red-handed, but she now had a burning desire to find out who the other woman was. She believed that if she figured that out she could eliminate her from the equation. She couldn't stop the tears from streaming out of her eyes, or the smoldering sensation she now felt in her heart. But, instead of making a fool out of herself or causing him to walk out, she headed back downstairs as if she'd never head anything. Grabbing her cell phone and walking outside for some privacy, she dialed Kiki. She needed her words of wisdom to steer her in the right direction. After three rings Kiki picked up. Diamond could barely hear her over the loud music in the background.

"Hey, girl. I know you just left but do you have a minute? I could really use your advice right now," Diamond yelled into the receiver.

"Hold on," Kiki said, turning down the music in her car. "Hello?"

"Hey, Kiki, it's me, Diamond. Are you busy? I could really use your advice on something," she repeated.

"Oh hey, girl, what's up? I have a few minutes before I get to the club."

"Girl, I think Black is cheating on me again," she said after a sigh and a short pause.

"What? Why do you think that?" she asked, shocked.

"Because I confronted him right after you left about the distance between us and of course he denied it. Well then he goes upstairs and makes a phone call. I can tell by the way he was responding that he was talking to a woman."

"That doesn't mean he's cheating, D. In his line of work I'm sure that he has to talk to women."

"Yeah, but not like that!" she replied.

"Not like what?"

"He was whispering and shit. Who does that if they aren't trying to hide something?" Diamond yelled.

"I don't know, D, but I mean unless you have concrete proof I wouldn't just go accusing him of anything."

"Damn, Kiki, I *thought* you were my friend. If I didn't know any better I'd think that you were taking his side."

"Diamond, what are you talking about? I'm not taking his side. I'm just saying be rational here," Kiki responded with annoyance in her tone.

"You right, Kiki, sorry to bother you. I will talk to you later."

"Diamond," Kiki yelled to silence, as Diamond had already hung up the phone.

Diamond sat looking at the phone, shaking her head and hoping Kiki wouldn't call her back. She wasn't in the mood for any more lecturing. She was looking for a confidant and it was obvious that Kiki had changed during their time apart. She'd have to figure this one out on her own.

Chapter Six

Second Time Around

"Didn't I tell you I had you covered?" Romeo yelled over the loud music, which filled each corner of Club Onyx, an upscale gentleman's club in the south part of Philadelphia. "It has wall-to-wall bitches in here, man, and I'm not even talking about the stripper hoes. It's always more chicks in here than niggas, all of them ready to give up some ass." He laughed as he patted Reed on the shoulders and pushed him through the entrance of the club.

Reed immediately noticed the large stage, which had three poles and lights that lined the entire edge. On stage was a stripper who was skillfully working her way down the pole with her legs only. Reed shook his head, thinking how she had the strongest legs he'd ever seen. "Drop and Gimme 50" by Mike Jones was blasting though the sound system and the stripper known as Montana was working the stage, commanding the attention of every person, male and female, in the room. Reed was in a daze, almost frozen in the spot where his feet rested. Things had definitely changed; he certainly remembered this a lot different before getting booked.

"I see. I definitely can appreciate the abundance of pussy all up, down, and around here." Reed laughed and slapped Romeo a five. "Damn it feels good to be home." He continued to laugh, looking at the many asses jiggling and bouncing around. All he could do was shake his head in amusement. He felt like a kid in a candy store as his eyes wandered wildly and he held in drool that was slowly making its way to his lips. He was positive that any man who'd ever been in prison before could totally relate to the overwhelming feeling of adrenaline that was rushing through his veins.

"I got us a VIP section in the back," Romeo yelled, regaining Reed's attention.

The two men made their way over to the far rear corner of the club. The section was filled with plush upholstered armchairs and featured mini coffee tables that were adorned with white runners and large stainless-steel wine buckets. Some of the dancers walked around from hustler to hustler, grabbing a quick lap dance and a few dollars. Reed tried to hold it together as he didn't want his dick to begin bursting through his pants, bringing any extra attention, but he knew there wasn't any way he could make it through the night without it. Just the scent of the women was sending his senses wild.

"You all right, my nigga?" Romeo yelled, laughing at the faces Reed was making.

"Yeah, I'm good, just happy to be home you know. Can't wait to get up in some pussy, man, straight up." He laughed.

Romeo laughed at his friend, knowing exactly how he felt. He looked over at a dancer named Lucky as she entered the room with her stallion strut. Her caramel skin glistened in the colorful lighting, which flashed continuously from the ceiling. He was familiar with what she was capable of so he knew she was the perfect dancer to pay Reed some extra special attention for the evening. He raised his left hand in the air and waved her in their direction.

She nodded and began walking over to where the two men were seated. She bent over with her ass pointed up in the air and her long twenty-seven-inch ponytail extension draped to one side. Her pink thong panties were pulled down to the center of her ass, making it appear even plumper.

To Reed, the two round cheeks that sat inches away from his face looked as appetizing as a well done piece of porterhouse with a coat of Jack Daniel's Barbeque Sauce. He was tempted to reach out and grab it but he knew that was an offense that could have him ejected from the club. Instead, he sat patiently, waiting to see what Romeo had up his sleeve.

As Reed bobbed his head to the music he noticed Romeo pointing at him from his peripheral view. A few seconds later, Lucky was bending over, slowing whispering in his ear. "You wanna head to the private room with me?" she asked, seductively licking her lips.

Reed looked up at her and quickly replied, "No doubt," smiling from ear to ear. He stood from the chair, looking down at Lucky's ass, and began to follow her lead. Before walking out he reached behind his back and gave Romeo dap followed by a quick nod to thank him.

The two went into the back, where she was prepared to put on a show worth every penny of the five crisp one hundred dollar bills that Romeo had secretly slipped into her bra top. As he sat down he could feel the bass of the music vibrating through his body. The sexually charged track "Ride It" by Ciara appropriately boomed through the speakers.

Lucky stood in front of Reed and slowly began to gyrate her hips, swaying them from side to side, front to back, against the beat of the song. He instantly began to feel his dick throb and growing hard as a brick. The sensitivity of the head rubbing against his boxers and jeans kept him struggling to stay still in his seat. She moved closer to him and quickly turned around and moved to a seated position with both of her hands gripping the arms of the chair. The aroma of her perfume was tickling his nostrils with delight; even the scent of her hair smelled like something you'd want to eat for dessert. Lucky was a skilled dancer, not the run-of-the-mill ass shaker. She moved in ways he'd never seen or even knew were possible. He almost felt like a virgin staring at his first piece of ass. At one point, she even did a spilt over the chair handles and dipped her ass all the way down to the crotch of his pants and then up in front of his face. All he could imagine was him getting inside of her.

After twenty minutes of being tortured he thanked Lucky for the entertainment and began to head out of the room. He turned to look back at her but she had already disappeared through the door in the rear of the room. He shook his head and let out a laugh. He knew it was against the rules for the two to exchange numbers or make promises to meet at a later time. Though he was horny as hell he wasn't one to fuck up another person's cash flow, especially if he wasn't prepared to foot the bill. Shit, he had so much to do to get the streets back in order, a relationship, other than the one he thought he'd come home to, was the furthest thing from his mind.

He walked out and returned to the VIP section to find Romeo drunk as hell and grinning like a Cheshire cat. The sight was pretty comical and was just the laugh that he needed.

"So how was it?" he asked as he struggled to keep his balance.

"Torture, man." He laughed. "Naw, thanks, my dude, it was all good, just wish I could've taken her home."

"Awww come on. I know you ain't had no ass in a long time but you ain't T-Pain and you can't be falling in love with no damn stripper." He laughed.

"Love? Nigga, please, I'm just tryin'a get rid of two years worth of build up." He laughed.

"Too much information, nigga, way too much." Romeo laughed. "Let's get out of here. I'm hungry as hell. You wanna hit South Street Diner before I run you home?"

"Yeah, your drunk ass needs to sober up a bit anyway." He laughed. "Let's roll." He reached into his back pocket to grab his wallet to leave the hostess a tip. He felt a loose bill and retrieved it, not remembering putting any money into his pocket. He unfolded the crisp one hundred dollar bill and noticed a telephone number and a kiss in bright pink lipstick. Beneath the kiss was a note that read: "Call me . . . Olivia aka Lucky xoxo." He smiled, folded the bill, and put it back into his pocket. After tossing twenty dollars on the table he gave Romeo the signal to head toward the door.

The two men exited the club and walked toward Romeo's car. Before entering, Reed caught a glimpse of a black Range Rover riding by with twenty-four-inch rims and dark tinted windows. The car pulled over and the driver and two passengers emerged. The driver—a tall, thin, dark-skinned man—appeared to be in charge. You could tell by the attention that he commanded and the way that everyone followed his lead. Reed was used to being the center of attention so he found himself interested in the identity of the ringleader. Romeo looked up from flipping through his cell phone as the rumbling in his stomach was digging a hole into his back.

"Yo, what's up, man? I'm starving like Marvin over here," Romeo yelled.

"Who is this nigga over here? The tall black-ass nigga," Reed said, pointing across the street at the group of men who were now surrounded by groupies and wannabe hustlers.

"That's that nigga named Black, used to work for that nigga Kemp who got merked a couple of years back."

"Oh, yeah? I remember that shit clearly. When this nigga get all flashy and shit? I remember this nigga riding Kemp's coattail and shit," Reed said, as he remembered exactly who he was. Prior to his release, he thought the name and description that Johnny gave sounded familiar, but it wasn't until that moment when he could see his face that he realized exactly who he was. Thinking back, he'd even had a conversation or two with Black but he knew him by a different name. "Keyshawn or some shit like that," he said aloud.

"What?" Romeo asked, confused as to what the hell Reed was talking about.

"That's his real name, Keyshawn or some shit like that."

"Yo, why are you so fascinated with this nigga, man? I'm hungrier than a hostage and you over here worrying about a motherfucka's government. Don't tell me the pen got you turning sweet on me, man." Romeo laughed aloud.

"Man, fuck outta here. I'm far from sweet, nigga. I damn sure ain't fascinated either—I just got some shit to take care of that involves him, that's all," Reed replied, still focused on Black and his entourage. He took mental notes, trying to get as much information as he could without it being obvious that he had a hidden agenda. After a few more seconds of glaring he shook his head, turned to open the driver-side door, and sat down inside.

"Now can we go eat? I feel like I'm losing pounds by the second over here, nigga." Romeo laughed.

"Yeah, man." He shut the car door, turned the key in the ignition, and drove off. At that moment, he had two things on his mind—getting more information on Black and getting back on top, where he belonged. He was positive that this time around he would remain on top by any means necessary.

Chapter Seven

Forbidden Fruit

Black pulled up in front of a large single home in the Mount Airy section of the city. The house was aligned with neatly kept flowerbeds and trimmed green grass. The house, which he'd visited on many different occasions, looked different for some reason this particular day. *Maybe it's my mind playing tricks on me,* he thought. Over the past year he'd spent a lot of time here—time that he should have spent at home. Nothing about it was right but he couldn't seem to pull himself away no matter how much he wanted to. Just like anything else that was forbidden, it was always the most tempting and hard to resist. Black hadn't been strong enough to walk away. In the past, he'd made some choices that he regretted, especially those that brought pain to those he loved. He never did anything to intentionally hurt Diamond, but somehow he couldn't avoid it.

So, he sat there in his car, deep in thought, wondering if he should follow his heart and drive away or follow his mind and go inside. The way he saw it, the damage was already done and one more time wouldn't make any difference; if Diamond found out her reaction would still be the same. He sat there staring at the door of the house until the door opened and a female stood in the doorway waving in his direction. He took a deep breath and released a loud sigh before getting out of the car and heading her way.

"What took you so long? I thought I was going to end up wasting this outfit," Kiki said, pulling her robe open and revealing her Frederick's of Hollywood ensemble.

Licking his lips Black admired her curves. Her thirty-six double-D breasts were spilling out of her bra and her fat pussy was forcing a camel toe into her panties. He moved in close to her and touched her lips with his and grabbed her waist with both of his strong hands. She backed into the house, pulling him inside. Black used his feet to push the door closed as the two were engrossed in a French kiss. Piece by piece she began to undress him as they made their way toward the living room. As she unzipped his pants his rock-hard dick made its way through his boxers. She didn't waste any time getting down in a squatting position and wrapping her lips around it. She used both hands to massage the shaft in different directions while using her tongue to kiss the head.

"Damn," he moaned, enjoying every stroke. His knees almost buckled at one point, as Kiki knew exactly how to make him feel good; not that Diamond didn't, but sex with Kiki always went to a level he hadn't yet experienced with Diamond. Most likely, that was because everything about it was so wrong.

Kiki continued her rendition of the greatest blowjob ever while Black fought to remain on his feet. He struggled to keep himself from an early eruption by focusing on something else but after a few minutes of fighting he pulled himself from her grips.

"What's wrong? Too much for you?" She laughed.

"Come here," he said, pulling her from her squatting position. She smiled and quickly obliged.

Standing face to face they stared at each other silently with different thoughts: Kiki thinking about the relationship she wished she had with Black; and Black thinking about the pain that this would cause Diamond. Kiki looked in his eyes and could tell what he was thinking and she didn't feel sorry for her actions. Diamond had done so much wrong to so many people she truly believed that she didn't deserve a man like Black. Black was the kind of man she needed in her life. Over a year ago when this affair began she felt that she belonged with him, but with most men, there was just something about Diamond that kept him holding on to her. Regardless of her faults and flaws Black loved her just as much today as he did when he married her. Kiki knew she didn't possess what he wanted in a wife so she was willing to settle for whatever he would give.

"Kiki, look," Black began to speak.

"Black, I understand," she began to respond but was cut off by Black quickly putting his right index finger in front of her lips.

"Don't talk, just listen. I enjoy being with you and I don't ever want you to think that I don't. Mentally, this is draining me because I love my wife and it's really no reason for me to be treating her this way. Now, I care about you and I'm not saying that I want this to stop, however, I don't want you to think that I am going to leave her because I'm not." Black paused. "I don't want to hurt either of you."

Regardless of the way things appeared he was sincere. He didn't want to hurt either of them, and though it might have seemed stupid he knew getting them back on track as friends was probably the only way he could keep this affair a secret. By keeping them close, he could keep them both at arm's reach.

"I get it, Black. I never expected you to leave her," she lied. "I'm happy with what I can get. Now, can we stop with all of the chatter and get to screwing? If I get any wetter there is going to be a puddle on the floor." She laughed.

Black laughed with her and then leaned in to kiss her. Feeling satisfied with their arrangement, his hands made their way to her wet mound. He parted her lips with his index and ring finger and slowly massaged her clit with his middle finger. She moaned as delight oozed from her skin and filled the room. Black's dick remained hard and would occasionally bump up against her stomach as he fingered her wet pussy.

"Fuck me please," she begged, eager to feel him inside of her.

Without a word Black picked her up and palmed her ass cheeks as she wrapped her legs around his waist. Using his strong leg muscles to stand firm, he guided her up and down on his dick with force. Her ass slapped up against him loudly echoing in the quiet room. "Oh, Black, shit." She moaned.

"Is it good, baby?" he asked, gaining speed.

"Yes," she yelled.

"Do you like it?" he asked.

"Yes, I like it," she screamed.

"Do you love it?"

"Yes, I love it," she answered with a moan and a sigh. She could feel her body began to shake as he hit her G-spot continuously. Her legs were tightly wrapped around his waist. He could barely move she was holding him so tightly.

"How does it feel?" he asked. It turned him on knowing that he was doing all that he could do to make her reach her sexual peak. He loved conformation and she loved giving it to him.

"Black, I'm about to cum," she yelled.

"Yeah?" he asked while forcing his dick deeper inside of her.

She wrapped her arms around his neck and stuck her tongue into his mouth, forcing a kiss. Her body bounced up and down until she erupted and her juices were running down the shaft of his dick. The warmness of it caused him to follow suit as he quickly let loose all that he'd tried to hold on to. His legs weakened and he grabbed hold of the sofa to brace himself as all of his energy left his body. She unwrapped her legs and slid off of him. Still facing him, she thought about having the moment last a little longer, but the reality of it all was that her would be leaving and going home to his wife.

"Black, I love you," she said without thinking. She'd wanted to tell him those words for months but had never mustered up the courage to say it. After she said it and he stood silent, she felt as if she'd made a mistake.

Black stood there, staring at her for a few seconds without replying. He hadn't figured out what this thing was but he couldn't hide the way he felt about her any longer. "I love you too, Kiki," he spoke softly.

A huge smile formed on her face, as that was all she needed to hear. Without speaking another word Black picked up his clothing from the floor and headed to her bathroom to clean up before heading back out. Once in the bathroom he turned on the sink and stared at himself in the mirror. "What the fuck are you doing?" he asked himself aloud. He shook his head before grabbing a washcloth and soap. After he was dressed he kissed Kiki good-bye and went on his way.

His next destination was to meet up with Tommy. Earlier that day, Tommy left him a message saying they needed to meet and it was pretty urgent. Tommy was patiently waiting for Black in front of one of their safe houses when he arrived. He quickly exited the car and greeted him with their signature handshake.

"What's good, man? Sorry I'm late. I had to take care of girlfriend number two," he joked.

"You a wild boy," Tommy said as he shook his head. "Let's step over here for a second." He nodded his head over to the left of the building.

The two walked over to the dimly lit side door where they could talk in private but still be seen by the armed gunmen who watched the doors.

"So what's the deal? What so urgent that I had to rush over here?" Black asked immediately, as he was anxious to hear what Tommy had to say.

"You remember the nigga named Reed from up west? He got locked up a couple years ago in that big-ass bust the feds did up Wynnfield."

Black shook his head, trying to picture him. "Naw, I don't remember him."

"You remember, the nigga who had the young nigga Brook who used to run with him. He over Jersey now."

"Oh yeah, I remember now, I thought that nigga name was Chance or some shit."

"It is but they call him Reed. Well he just got out of jail and word on the street is he's trying to move in on our turf."

"Where the fuck you hear that?"

"A bunch of niggas, you know I always got my ear to the streets. I don't know if it's true but I'm saying that's what I hear. I just don't want this nigga to creep up on us and we're not prepared."

Black stood there, rubbing his hands across his beard deep in thought. If the information was true they needed to come up with a plan to throw him off.

"So what do you wanna do?" Tommy asked, so anxious he could barely stand still.

"I'm thinking, calm down." Black raised his voice an octave.

"I can't calm down when a nigga is trying to wreck the shit I live off of."

"Being all hype is what these niggas want. All they need is to catch you slipping and bam! Your ass is grass. You gotta use your head, man. I know you're upset. Don't think I'm not, I just like to think logically and come up with a strategy rather than going in with my heart all angry and shit," Black replied, trying to calm Tommy down. He hoped that Tommy would use his head.

"I get it, Black, I'm just trying to see what you want me to do. I don't trust these niggas. I feel like they are planning some shit and I just don't want our shit to crumble. We've worked too hard to let a nigga walk in and take what's rightfully ours."

"Could you set up a meeting with your sources? At least that way I can hear all that they've heard."

"Yeah, I can do that. When do you wanna meet?"

"As soon as possible. If you can get them together by tomorrow night I can swing by here and then we can go from there."

"All right, cool. I will just hit you up tomorrow when I confirm everything."

"Cool," Black said, reaching out to shake Tommy's hand. Tommy entered the building while Black got into his car to drive home. He grabbed his 9 mm handgun from under the seat and placed it on his lap. In the event someone approached he would be prepared for them. Now more than ever he was going to have to look over his shoulders, at least until they were certain things were under control.

Chapter Eight

A Game of Chess

Reed sat outside of a large warehouse, patiently waiting for his seven o'clock meeting. Every so often he'd glance at the time, which was brightly displayed on the car radio, before turning his attention back toward the huge grey metal door guarded by two tall, husky men. Both wore all black from head to toe including their leather gloves, Skullies, and Timberland hiking boots. The two men were engrossed in conversation but aware of their surroundings at the same time. The clock read six forty-five the last time Reed checked but he couldn't stop himself from looking again at six forty-eight. He wasn't being impatient, but more so anxious to get this over with.

The past three weeks had been all about this vendetta that Johnny had against Black. He hadn't even been able to focus on his own plans, or even enjoy his freedom. As he began to think about all the things he wanted to do once this was all over with, two men emerged from the warehouse doors. After shaking the hands of the two guards the men began to make their way over to Reed's car, which was parked on the opposite side of the street. Both of the men entered the car, one in the passenger seat and one in the back. Reed turned on the car and immediately began pulling out of the parking spot and heading down the dimly lit street.

"Any word from Johnny?" Reed asked, looking over at the man in his passenger seat.

"Yeah, the thirteenth is the day. We can get in, take care of this nigga, Black, and get the fuck outta there," Justice replied in a deep, raspy tone. Justice was the only one of the two who Reed kept in contact with. The other passenger, Dex, was there in the event that things went awry.

"So what about the girl, Diamond?" Reed questioned. From the conversations that he'd had with Johnny while behind bars, she was the main target but, somehow, the focus seemed to have shifted totally on Black.

"What about her?" Justice asked, turning toward Reed.

"I'm saying, what are we supposed to do about her? I thought she was supposed to be taken care of as well, so I'm a tad bit confused here."

"Listen, I'm just as clueless as you, dog. Johnny told me that we needed to get the money and get rid of Black, that's all."

Reed shook his head and kept quiet to avoid saying the wrong thing. This was exactly the kind of shit he didn't want to happen. Most importantly, this was exactly why he had a backup plan. There was something about the two men that didn't sit well with him. It was almost as if he could feel the knife touching his back ready to stab him as soon as he was caught slipping. He didn't plan on going out like a sucker, nor did he plan on being used as a pawn in Johnny's game of chess.

"All right, well, what time is this all supposed to take place?"

"We'll figure that out next week. What we need to take care of right now is figuring out who is taking care of what." Justice changed his tone to one of seriousness.

Reed kept his composure, knowing that his responses could be the difference between life and death. Losing his cool would only cause turmoil and he didn't trust either of them as far as he could throw them.

As Justice sat across from Reed he tried to read his movements and expressions. Johnny always told him to study people, especially those you did dirt with. You never wanted a man who could wreck your life to have one up on you. You always needed to pay attention even when everyone else didn't. Though he didn't know Reed personally, he'd sat with Johnny on many visits and he'd read a lot of letters where Reed was the topic of discussion. Though Johnny was just a teenager when he was locked away, being in prison turned him into a man quickly. It also made him more streetwise than he probably ever would have been at home.

"Okay, so what is it that I am supposed to do? Because you still haven't been clear about that, or really anything for that matter," Reed blurted after a few moments of silence.

"Your job is managing any bystanders, including the girl. We'll take care of getting the money and we'll take care of Black."

"And when will I get my cut?" Reed asked.

"We'll meet after a few days and give you what's owed to you."

Deep down Reed was feeling less comfortable by the second. He had to figure out a way to use his own man as backup. He knew something was wrong. It was just a gut feeling and most of the time his gut was right. By the way Justice spoke, it was almost as if he believed Reed was a pushover or a punk, and he was neither. Justice continued his speech as Reed sat quietly, thinking of his own strategy. After a few more minutes of driving and conversation Reed was pulling back up in front of the warehouse where he'd picked them up. The two men exited the car and Justice quickly shook Reed's hand before walking across the street toward his own car, which was parked on the corner.

Reed watched as he opened the door and got inside. He was thinking that he'd gotten himself into a situation that might not have been in his best interest. Thinking back to the day that he agreed to taking care of this for Johnny, he wasn't 100 percent sure of what made him say yes. Yeah, he wanted the money, but he didn't need it. Things were pretty much set for him financially. Was it greed? Or, was it just the excitement of it all? He asked himself these questions over and over again because he was the type of man who needed to make sense of anything that he did, even if it didn't make sense to anyone else.

As he began to drive off his cell phone rang and the name "Lucky" flashed across his screen. He'd called her a few times since the night that she'd first given him her number, but he'd been so busy the past few weeks that he hadn't gotten around to actually hooking up with her. He lifted the phone from his lap and pressed the green call button and cleared his throat before speaking.

"Hello," he said in a deep baritone.

"Is Reed available?" Her voice oozed sexiness through the receiver.

"This is Reed, who's this?" he asked, though he'd already saved her number and knew who she was before he'd even answered.

"This is Lucky, the dancer you met at the club," she reminded him.

"Oh, okay. I erased your number from my phone when you never called me back," he lied.

"I'm sorry, I was working like crazy. Trying to pay my tuition for school. It wasn't intentional at all. I definitely wanted to talk to you."

"Is that right?" he asked, smiling but maintaining a serious tone.

"Definitely, I have never given my number to a customer. First of all, it's against the rules, but besides that, you're the sexiest man I've seen in a very long time."

Reed shook his head, knowing that she'd probably spit the same game to other men on different occasions. Here she was, a stripper trying to act like an innocent schoolgirl. There was something about her that intrigued him and because of that he entertained the conversation a little longer than he normally would.

"So, what are you getting into tonight? I'm assuming that you're going to work."

"Actually, I didn't work tonight. I took a 'me day' for some much-needed relaxation," she replied, hoping that his next question would involve meeting him and hanging out for the evening.

"Relaxation, huh? So I guess that means your full of energy then?" He laughed.

"Yup, Energizer Bunny!" She let out a girlish giggle.

"Well, what are you trying to get into? You feel like hanging out?"

"Depends on what you have in mind."

"Well, I'm a man who likes to surprise. If you're not up to it, I totally understand, but if I tell you everything you won't appreciate the details as much."

"Well, how much detail could you possibly whip up on such short notice?" she asked, shaking her head. She wasn't impressed but she was eager to hear more. She got comfortable in her seat and waited for him to answer.

"You'd be surprised what a man like me could do with a little bit of time. I can make the impossible very possible. Believe me," he replied with confidence. He didn't have a clue what he wanted to do but he had to make it sound good if he wanted to keep her attention. "And if you don't know about me now, you will by the end of the night. That's for damn sure." He laughed.

"Well, we're wasting time talking. I should be getting ready for you to pick me up," she said with a huge smile on her face. She couldn't remember the last time a man had made her this anxious to see him. She couldn't wait to get off the phone to hurry upstairs to pick the flyest outfit in the closet.

"You're absolutely right. Well you get ready, text me your address, and I will see you in an hour. Is that enough time or are you one of those two-to-three-hour women?"

"Please, I am naturally beautiful. I can be ready in less than an hour and still look like I stepped off of a magazine spread. I'm the shit, boy; don't doubt me." She laughed.

"All right then, I'll see you in a bit."

"Okay, I'll be waiting."

Lucky sent her address to his phone as requested before running to the bathroom to jump in the shower. She made sure to pay extra attention to the hot spots in the event that things turned physical. She lathered her body with her

Victoria's Secret Pure Seduction body wash a total of four times. She even completed a smell test before exiting the shower to be sure that things were in order.

She glanced at the clock and realized that she had used up twenty minutes in the shower. She didn't know much about but Reed, but if he was punctual she'd hate to keep him waiting, especially after proclaiming how fast she could be prepared.

She ran down the hall to her bedroom and rummaged through her drawer to find underwear. Wanting the perfect set, she'd knocked most of what was in the drawer onto the floor. She settled on a black lace bra and thong. Black was always sexy, especially on her size-eight curvy frame. She'd been blessed by the best with a full thirty-eight double-D cup, twenty-seven-inch waist, and forty-two-inch hips. A Coke bottle didn't have shit on this brick house. It didn't stop at the great frame either—she also had a face as beautiful as a porcelain doll. Her skin was a glowing caramel and remained blemish free. Unlike some of the other dancers at the club, Lucky could quickly transform from the stage to the classy woman you would love to carry on your arm or to meet Mama. Naturally, she was great in bed, using her dancing and stage skills to make a man lose his mind. She worked hard at perfecting her lovemaking skill to ensure that her future husband would be satisfied.

After slipping into her all-black Badgely Mischka mid-thigh-length dress, which generously accentuated her curves, and putting on her Christian Louboutin glitter daffodil pumps, she was dressed to impress without a minute to spare. As promised, Reed rang her bell at exactly one hour, and Lucky loved a man of his word. She hurried to the door but stopped just short of it to look at herself in the floor-length mirror once more to be sure that everything was still in place. Once she was satisfied with her look she opened the door with a huge smile and one hand placed on her hip.

Reed looked her up and down and rubbed the hair on his chin before speaking. "Damn, you look even better with clothes on. I didn't know that shit was even possible." He laughed while Lucky did a quick spin to give him a full 360-degree view. "I would've planned something a little more fancy if I knew you would come out with your Sunday's best on." He continued to laugh.

"This isn't hardly my Sunday's best. More like a Saturday night special, and I can change if I'm gonna be wasting a good outfit," she said, twisting her lip.

"I was just playing. Come on now, you need that outfit just to walk with me." He laughed. "But I wouldn't have you get all dressed up for nothing. I'm not that dude."

"I would hope not." She smiled, feeling a little better.

"Did you pack an overnight bag?"

"An overnight bag? Who said I was staying overnight with you?"

"I did. Trust me, after a night with me, you won't want to come home tonight. Hell you may not ever want to come home for real, for real."

"Oh, *really?*" she asked. She wasn't sure if it was confidence or arrogance; either way, it was a turn-on. Reed stood there, silent, as Lucky stared at him waiting for a response. After a few seconds she broke the silence. "Okay, give me a few minutes. I'll go pack a bag."

Reed laughed to himself as Lucky disappeared into the house to gather enough things to last a weekend. She made sure to grab sexy underwear and smell-goods. Reed was patiently waiting for her when she returned to the door with her bag in hand.

For most of the ride the two rode in silence until Lucky initiated an inevitable conversation. "So, Mr. Reed, I've never seen you around before. Where were you hiding?"

"I wasn't hiding, I was locked up," he answered honestly. "Got locked up on a drug charge but that's the past, you know. I'm home now, back on top where I need to be."

"I see. I was about to ask how you can just come home to a fly-ass car, clothes, and money to throw around like there's no tomorrow."

"Well, I have good friends."

"What about a woman? Do you have one of those?"

He laughed. "I was waiting for that one, actually. I have a wife, but when I came home she served my ass with divorce papers. Soon as I was away she jumped on the next thing smoking, shipped my daughter off to her relatives, and rolled out to live the glamorous life."

"Wow." Lucky shook her head in disbelief.

"Yeah, wow is right. That's what I said when I came home and found out. That was my welcome home gift. But it's all good. But enough about me, let's hear about you, Miss Lucky. How did you end up dancing for a living?"

"Money is the root of that evil of course. I needed money for college. I wasn't blessed with parents who could send me to school or a man who had the funds to assist so I had to get it on my own. I'll be done with school in eight months and I can say that I don't have any student loans to pay back when I graduate."

"Do you like your job?"

"Of course not, but it pays the bills," she said with attitude.

"Don't shoot me, I was just asking an honest question. I mean, there are people out there who actually like what they do. No disrespect, you do your job very well, so usually when women take the job that serious, it's because they like it."

"Well for me, anything that I decide to do I make sure I am the best at it. If I'm not going to put my best foot forward then I'm not going to do it."

"I respect that. I respect that one hundred percent," Reed responded.

"Good, 'cause I didn't wanna have to shoot you," she said before they both burst into laughter.

Soon they were pulling up in front of Reed's home and parking in the driveway. While Lucky had expected going out to a nice restaurant for dinner she wasn't surprised that he'd bought her here instead. She shook her head, thinking, *why the hell did I think anything different in the first place?* She went to exit the car and Reed stopped her.

"I'm just going to drop off your bag, grab some money, and then we'll be on our way."

"Okay," she replied, caught off guard but in a good way. She was immediately excited and anxious about what he was planning. Here she was giving up on him before he had a chance to show and prove.

Reed returned to the car a few minutes later and began the drive to their next destination. A half-hour later they arrived at a beautiful restaurant in Rittenhouse Square in downtown Philadelphia. The small, cozy restaurant was just the atmosphere that they needed to tip off a romantic evening. The night had been going well so far and both of them were looking forward to ending it with a bang, both figuratively and literally. The restaurant was sparsely filled with couples of all different ages and nationalities.

The couple was seated and immediately served a bottle of the best champagne. Lucky wasn't a huge fan of champagne but she figured she'd make an exception for the special occasion. She was very interested in finding out more about him. To her, he was mysterious and she'd always wanted that in a man. She watched his every move and listened to his every word as they went through the three courses of their meal. Though she'd enjoyed the dinner and conversation she was excited to move on to the next portion of their evening.

Soon the two were on their way back to Reed's house, both anticipating what was next. Reed was planning on giving her every bit of the energy that he'd had backed up for the past two years and Lucky, well, she was planning on receiving it.

Chapter Nine

Foolin' Around

"So what did you find out?" Black asked Tommy as he sat down in the plush leather chair, which sat behind his large cherry-wood desk. Three days ago he learned of Reed, a man who was on a mission to come up in the drug game. He wasn't scared but he hated to be blind in any situation, especially one that threatened his life. He couldn't rest easy until any potential threat was eliminated.

"Nothing really. I really don't see him as a threat. He isn't really making any noise. He's trying to come up but not takeover nothing that we own," Tommy replied while sitting down in the chair that sat opposite Black.

"So you ain't found out nothing in three days? That's all you have to tell me?" Black asked, visibly annoyed.

"I asked around, man, nobody knows anything. Dude is pretty low-key, he doesn't cause too much noise." Tommy leaned forward in the chair.

"I hope you're right. I really do." Black shook his head. "You know niggas are constantly trying to move in and attack. I have a family, man. I need to be here for them and I can't watch my own back. That's what I have you for. I feel like you've been slipping lately."

"Now I'm slipping? I'm the one who brought this shit to your attention. I know this shit is stressful, man, but come on—there is no need to start throwing unnecessary jabs. I've always had your back."

"I'm just saying, you should be up on this shit. There shouldn't be any room for mistakes if you cross all your t's and dot all your i's," Black yelled.

"There won't be any mistakes, Black," Tommy responded, raising his voice. He was frustrated with Black's tone. Not once did he ever think Black would doubt his ability to handle business. Regardless of the situation, he had always come through. He wanted to just chalk it all up to stress but something inside of him wouldn't allow him to. Honestly, he felt like his time with Black was almost up and, soon, he'd have to do his own thing. "I don't understand you, man. Who was the one who saved you and your wife? Me! I have always been there to shield you from harm." Tommy was now standing as his adrenaline began to pump through his veins.

"Yo, sit down, man, you taking this shit too personal. This shit ain't about no friendships or any other shit like that. This is about my life and my family. I can't allow a nigga to move in and take what's mine. Yes, you were there in the past but back then you took your job more seriously. If I'm wrong then, okay, I'll be a man and apologize, but right now this shit is business. I need to know more about this nigga and his master plan. Now you can either help me or keep bitching, one or the other," Black said, pounding his closed fist against the desk.

Tommy stood on the opposite side of the office and stared at Black. His stare was direct and his eyes were piercing. It was almost as if he could see right through Black. So many thoughts were running through his head. He was growing angrier by the second, but he tried as hard as he could to conceal any obvious signs of it. He stood steady in the same place for a few more minutes before walking back over to the chair where he'd originally been seated, and flopped down in it.

Black shook his head as he wondered what Tommy was thinking. He was sure by the look on Tommy's face that it wasn't something positive, but it didn't scare him or ruffle his feathers in the least bit. He had to worry about himself and his family—babysitting wasn't an option.

Tommy was still quiet, trying to figure out what to say next. He didn't want this to turn into a war but he didn't want to seem like a bitch either. Though he worked for Black he wasn't a servant and wasn't going to bow down like one either.

"So what are you planning on doing?" Black asked, restarting the conversation that had sat dormant for the past five minutes.

Tommy shook his head before speaking. "I'm going to do the best that I can to find out what's going on."

"All right, well, I'll get up with you later. I need to go take care of some other shit," Black said before walking around the desk and giving Tommy dap and heading toward the door.

As he walked toward his car he noticed a black Mercedes near the corner with tinted windows. He watched the car as he got inside of his car. He refused to move and be followed if something was up. He wanted to make sure they knew he wasn't afraid or running scared. After a few minutes the car pulled out of the parking and sped off down the street and around the corner. Because of the dark tinted windows, he couldn't see who was inside. After all of the shit that he'd been through the previous year, shit like this instantly put him on edge. A few moments later, his cell phone rang, breaking the silence and startling him. Looking down at the caller ID, Diamond's name flashed across the screen.

"Hello," he said dryly.

"Where are you? I thought you were coming straight home, Black. It's been three hours since I last spoke to you."

"Diamond, I'm a grown-ass man, okay? Stop clocking me like a fucking child."

"What the fuck is your problem lately, Black? Is it that bitch you're cheating on me with?" she screamed into the phone.

"Good-bye, Diamond," Black said, attempting to end the conversation and avoid the inevitable conversation. He knew it was only a matter of time before Diamond would figure it out but he wasn't in the mood for the discussion at the moment.

"Oh so you're gonna hang up on me? That's real mature, Black. I know what you're doing and I don't deserve it. I haven't done anything but try to be the best wife I can be and this is how you repay me," she yelled as her voice began to quiver.

Black was quiet, not knowing how to respond. She was right, she didn't deserve it, and the reason that he was wrapped up in an affair didn't have anything to do with her. She had been a good wife but for a reason that he couldn't quite explain he slipped again.

"Cat got your tongue?" she asked with evident pain in her voice. She wanted to burst into tears but her pride wouldn't let her show him how this was affecting her.

"Diamond, I'm really not in the mood for this shit right now. It doesn't really matter what I say, you still won't believe me, so what's the point?" he responded.

"You know what, Black, fuck it! Have a good night!" She hung up the phone and screamed. She was furious. Deep down she'd hoped that he would respond differently and reassure her that his heart still belonged to her. Unfortunately, the conversation went left and she felt even worse than she did before she called.

Black looked at the phone and shook his head. Instead of going home, he made a U-turn and took the on-ramp to I-76 to head to Kiki's house for the evening. He pulled up in front of her house twenty minutes later and dialed her cell phone to be sure she didn't have any company before ringing the doorbell.

"Hello," she breathed into the phone.

"Did I wake you?" Black asked, noticing the harshness in her voice.

"Yeah, but it's okay. What's up?" She perked up after hearing the sound of his voice. She was always happy to hear from him.

"I'm outside. I don't feel like going home tonight. Diamond's in bitch mode."

"Okay, I'm coming down," she replied before getting out of bed. She walked downstairs and opened the door wearing only a T-shirt and a red thong. Black smiled when he saw her. It was almost as if she'd taken Diamond's place keeping a smile on his face. As she backed into the house he grabbed her around the waist and pulled her close to him. Her skin was soft as silk as his large hands caressed both of her exposed cheeks.

"I see somebody missed me." She laughed.

"I definitely missed you," he replied, feeling a relief from all the drama at home.

"How much?" she asked, backing away from him. "This much?" she asked, holding her arms apart, creating a space with her hands.

Black took off his jacket and set it down on the chair near the entrance of the living room. Gently, he pushed Kiki back so that her butt rested on the arm of the sofa. In a swift motion, he got on his knees and pulled her thong to the side, revealing her perfectly shaved pussy. His thick tongue licked her clit with just enough pressure to send her into an instant orgasm. She'd never erupted so prematurely but her feelings for Black mixed with adrenaline made it almost impossible to hold it back. She rested her legs on his shoulders and nestled his head in place. He sopped up all of her juices and French kissed her lips, making a loud smacking sound. Slipping his right index and middle finger inside of her, he continued to suck on her clit while massaging her G-spot with his fingers. She rocked her hips and used her hands to brace herself as she pressed her pussy harder into his face.

"Right there, baby, that's it," she moaned, letting him know that he was in the right spot. She leaned back and lifted her cheeks slightly to give him more room. He removed his finger from her wet tunnel and used his hands to wrap them around her thighs and pull them farther apart. Hearing her delight only fueled his fire and he used every trick in the book to give her exactly what she was yearning for. "Oh shit, Black," she screamed as she reached yet another orgasm and her body began to shake uncontrollably.

Black pulled himself away and stood up from the floor with a huge smile and a rock-hard dick trying to make its way out of his boxers and jeans. Kiki still had her eyes closed, trying to regain her composure. He laughed a little at the sight of it, which turned him on even more. He quickly loosened his belt and unzipped his pants, allowing them to drop to the floor. With her legs open wide he moved back in close to her and touched her lips with his before grabbing hold of her neck and ramming his long dick into her pussy, causing an instant release of juices from inside of her. He fit inside of her like a glove as he maneuvered his way around her insides like a well-lit racetrack. He pulled himself in and out of her slowly and made sure to push every inch of himself inside of her. She continued to moan as he remained focused on reaching his sexual peak. From the floor his cell phone began to ring but both of them ignored it. He figured that it would be Diamond and he wasn't going to let her ruin the nut that he was anticipating. He pumped harder and with each stroke Kiki moaned louder. She wrapped her arms around his neck to pull him closer and used her tongue to lick his left ear.

"Oh shit," he moaned, feeling all of his energy rushing to the head of his dick.

She continued to suck and lick on his ear as he fucked her as hard as he could. Within minutes he was releasing what felt like eight ounces of cum inside of her. The head of his dick was instantly so sensitive that he didn't want to back away. She laughed, knowing why he was still holding on to her so tight.

"What's so funny?" he asked, keeping as still as he possibly could.

"You, sir." She laughed, moving her hips and forcing him to quickly pull his semi-soft dick from her pussy.

"That's not funny at all," he replied before sitting down on the chair.

His cell phone began to ring again. He grabbed his pants from the floor to retrieve it. Looking down at the caller ID he wasn't surprised to see Diamond's name flashing across the screen.

"Is that who I think it is?" Kiki asked curiously. She could tell by the look on his face that he wasn't happy and figured that it could only be her.

"Yeah, she keeps calling back and I swear I don't feel like fighting with her."

"Well, turn the phone off then," she suggested.

"I can't turn it off. You know I get business calls at all different times of the night."

"Well, answer it then, Black. She's not going to stop calling so you might as well get it over with."

He took a deep breath before answering the phone with an obvious attitude. "What?" he yelled.

"Is that how you answer the phone for your wife?"

"Yeah, when you're getting on my nerves," he replied. "What do you want, Diamond?"

"Are you coming home?"

"No, Diamond, I will see you tomorrow. I need time alone tonight." *Click.*

Diamond looked at the phone, hoping that he didn't just hang up on her. Realizing that the call was ended tears began to drop from her eyes. She realized that she was losing him and she wasn't prepared for that.

She went upstairs and looked in on her sleeping daughter. *How can he do this to us?* The situation was turning out to be a lot harder to figure out than she'd expected. Either way, she wasn't going down without a fight. She closed the door and walked to her bedroom, where she crawled into bed and soon fell asleep clutching her cell phone in her hand, hoping that he would call.

Chapter Ten

Breath of Fresh Air

"What's on your mind?" Reed asked, looking at Lucky as she lay looking up at the ceiling.

"Nothing really," she replied. "Just happy that's all." She smiled. Being with him the past few weeks was turning out to be more exciting than she'd expected. She'd never met a man like Reed who was so strong yet so caring. He always made sure to keep a smile on her face and she could appreciate that. Even in his thug state he was gentle.

Reed sat up from the bed and stared her in the eyes. He was trying to read her mind, knowing that there was more to her silence than she was letting on. She was beautiful both inside and out, unlike his estranged wife, Raquel. He saw something in her that he hadn't seen with any other woman. She wasn't afraid to let him in, almost as if she'd never had her heart broken.

Most women would resist, especially with a man like him, who could have almost any woman that he wanted. Lucky was almost the perfect woman and he didn't plan on letting her go anytime soon.

"So what are you so happy about?" Reed finally asked, breaking the brief silence.

"Everything. My life is going great now and it's all because of you." She smiled.

"I'm just glad that you're allowing me into your heart. For real. I know things with us are moving fast, but when something feels this good, I don't see a reason to slow down," he said sincerely. "I mean what I say, so I hope that you don't think I'm gassing you up."

She laughed. "No, I don't believe that. You haven't lied to me. Well, I haven't caught you in a lie, so I can only trust that what you are saying is the truth."

"Caught me?" He laughed. "I'm as real as they come, you can believe that."

He leaned in to kiss her, satisfied with the conversation and where the relationship was going. She met his lips without the slightest bit of resistance. The two locked lips for a full two minutes before his cell phone began blaring, rudely interrupting their moment of passion. Reed ignored the annoying ring tone and slowly forced his tongue through her lips and began massaging her tongue. The phone continued to ring, forcing them to break their connection.

"You might as well just see who it is. Doesn't look like they are planning to stop calling," Lucky said, hoping that answering the call would give them whatever it was they were calling for.

Without looking at the caller ID, Reed answered the phone with an attitude. "Hello," he yelled.

"Is this Reed?" A deep male voice boomed through the receiver.

Reed pulled the phone away from his ear to glance at the caller ID, which conveniently read, "Unknown." Returning the phone to his ear he added extra bass to voice before responding, "Who wants to know?" His face was balled in a knot.

"Damn, it's been that long?" The caller laughed. "Well, this is Brook and, believe me, I'm not calling to reminisce. I need to find out what's holding up your signature on those divorce papers." He finished with an even tone.

"Are you fucking kidding me?" He removed the phone from his ear once more and looked at it with anger written all across his face. "I can't believe that you have the fucking balls to call me with this bullshit!" He shook his head. "I didn't even have beef with you about her 'cause I don't give a fuck about that trifling-ass bitch. That shit doesn't have anything to do with you so you need to stay in your fucking place!" he yelled, furious, as spit flew from the sides of his mouth. He stood up from the bed and began pacing the floor.

"My place? Yeah, all right, muthafucker. This ain't back when you got booked. You don't run shit, nigga. I'm tryin'a let you breathe but if you want to make shit difficult I can make it so she'll be filing for a death certificate instead."

Reed was screaming and pointing at the phone. He was practically foaming at the mouth by this point. "Try it then, muthafucker. You know where to find me." He ended the call and slammed the phone down on the bed.

Lucky sat up, almost afraid to speak.

"This nigga wants to fuck with me? I will kill that muthafucker and that bitch," he yelled, pacing. He walked back over to the bed and grabbed his cell phone and immediately dialed Romeo on the phone.

"Yo, I need some niggas to take care of this muthafucker, Brook. This nigga had the fucking balls to call my phone threatening me and shit."

"What?" Romeo yelled back.

"Yo, I'm so fucking pissed right now, I want this nigga buried. You hear me, man? Six fucking feet under," he yelled.

"All right, calm down. Where you at?"

"I'm home."

"I'll be over there in a half-hour. Just sit tight, all right? I don't wanna talk too much on this phone," Romeo replied as he grabbed his jeans from the back of his chair and began to put them on.

"All right," Reed replied before putting the phone back down.

Lucky was still sitting up at the top of the bed, quiet as a mouse. She was afraid to speak for fear that she'd say the wrong thing and piss him off even more.

Reed turned to look at her and immediately noticed the fear in her eyes. He walked over to her and sat down beside her on the bed. "I'm sorry about that, okay, baby? I don't want you to worry about that or me. Everything's gonna be okay." He softly rubbed her right thigh.

"I don't want anything to happen to you," she spoke softly, holding back the tears that were forming in the wells of her eyes.

"Nothing is going to happen to me. Come here," he said, pulling her close to him and wrapping his arms around her.

She breathed in his scent and felt secure in his arms. Things were going too good for everything to be snatched away. She was just getting used to life with him.

"Do you have somewhere that I can take you while I go take care of this? I don't feel comfortable leaving you here alone right now."

"Yes, you can take me to my aunt's house."

"Okay, get dressed and I'll be downstairs," he said before kissing her and getting up from the bed. He grabbed a pair of jeans from his closet and quickly threw them on with a pair of sneakers and headed downstairs to wait for Romeo.

Romeo arrived twenty minutes later along with Mike, one of their closest friends. They drove in silence until Lucky was dropped off and safely inside. Reed returned to the car stone-faced.

"So what do you want to do?" Romeo asked. He already felt like Brook would be a problem once Reed was home. He expected things to happen exactly the way that they were. After Reed was arrested, a lot in the street changed. Jealousy and egos quickly turned things upside down, forcing a separation in the crew. Brook was always known as a hothead but his attitude was always controllable with Reed around. Now that he could stand on his own financially and he had his trusty followers, he felt like he was untouchable. Dealing with Reed's wife was a slap in the face but Reed wasn't too concerned with that. The fact that she'd be out of his life was a good thing and it would give him great pleasure to watch her suffer when Brook was taken care of.

"You know what needs to be done. I can't have a fucking loose cannon running around while I'm trying to get shit back in order. I need this nigga to be officially wiped out. All the way off the fucking map! Whatever you have to do to handle that, handle it," he spoke, pounding his fist into his hand.

"I'll take care of it for sure. I was waiting for this day anyway. I already knew this nigga would start some shit. I was just waiting for your word," Romeo said while heading on to I-95.

"I can't believe that he really called you with that bullshit, man. This nigga really grew King Kong balls," Mike blurted as he shook his head. "I kinda wish I would've rocked that nigga to sleep years ago. Punk-ass muthafucker."

"It's all good though. I was having a nice night and shit wit' my baby and this bitch-ass nigga calls me." Reed spoke with a smile when thinking about Lucky.

"Sounds like shit's working out with her." Romeo laughed. "Your ass is really falling in love wit' a stripper." He chuckled.

"I guess I am." Reed smiled.

The car was now pulling up in front of one of their drop spots. All three men exited the car in sync and began to walk toward the entrance of the building. Without speaking, each of them nodded and gave dap to the two men guarding the door. Walking inside they headed toward the back of the building to the meeting room. Reed and Romeo entered the building alone while Mike remained outside in front of the bolted door. Reed and Romeo sat down at opposite sides of the table.

"You know I never thought shit would turn out the way that is has, man. It's crazy how your life can be turned upside down in the blink of an eye," Reed said, shaking his head.

"That's real shit, man, but you don't have to worry about this shit. I'm going to make sure that I take care of it." Romeo spoke with seriousness written across his face. He loved Reed like they were brothers and sisters and he vowed to always have his back. Most people looked at Romeo as if he was a servant of Black's, but the reality of the situation was that he'd never be his subordinate; he'd always been a partner. He was comfortable with his position and there wasn't a time that he felt the need to defend it.

"I should've listened to you, man, and never married that bitch. She is the true definition of hell on wheels." He laughed to mask his anger. He felt like screaming he was so pissed.

"Can't say I know how you feel but I know how it feels to want to kill a nigga," he responded.

"Well, I'm gonna jet so I can clear my mind. I just need to mentally put some shit in prospective." He stood from the table and walked around to the side of the table where Romeo was sitting. Romeo stood up from his seat to give him dap before tapping on the back of the door to let them know that they were about to come out.

"I'll get up with you in a few hours, all right?"

"Cool," Reed responded before walking out of the door and into the hallway.

Quietly, Reed headed out of the building and to the car, making sure to check his surroundings before pulling out of the parking spot. His mind was racing a mile a minute, thinking about everything that had led up to this very moment. Naturally, he regretted a lot of his decisions. He couldn't totally regret his decision to deal with Raquel since he'd gained a beautiful daughter he loved with all of his heart. He wasn't about to let her ruin his life and he'd do whatever he had to do to make it known.

Chapter Eleven

A Dose of Reality

Diamond sat on her sofa, looking out of the window. Her heart was filled with so much worry as the family she'd worked so hard to maintain was slowly slipping away. For the first time in her life she didn't know what to do. She felt like she was completely alone. Though she and Kiki were talking again, things still weren't the same. She figured that the time that they spent away from each other was the reason for the obvious distance. She thought back to some of her other friendships and as much as Kiki had bashed Mica's actions when it pertained to her, she was becoming a mirror image of her. She didn't even feel comfortable talking to Kiki, or any of her other friends for that matter, about her relationship with Black. She never wanted anyone to see it as an opportunity to slide in between, especially when things weren't at their best. The only person she'd been able to talk to was her mother, Pam.

Since meeting her a couple of years back, the two had actually become really good friends. When she first learned of her father's relationship with Pam and how she was the product of their affair, she didn't think that she would be able to truly embrace her as a mother. Learning of how her mother had stepped up and taken care of her husband's lovechild only made her respect and love her even more. When Nila, the only mother she'd known before meeting Pam, was ripped out of her life when she died of a drug overdose, she was bitter at the world. She was still angry that she hadn't been there to say good-bye. Eventually, she was able to forgive her grandmother for not telling her about her Nila's death until after the funeral, as she didn't have a callous bone in her body; she could never forgive her Aunt Cicely because every ounce of pain that she ever caused was intentional. She was positive that Cicely was the one who made it so that she wouldn't know about her death. Because of her jealousy, she showed nothing but hate for Diamond. This was her chance to see Diamond in pain and not only did she not tell her about the death and the funeral, she eliminated her from the obituary and brought her a copy just to rub it in her face. Pam had stepped in and been the shoulder that she could cry on and the person she could confide in when she need someone to talk to.

As she continued to stare off in thought she saw Pam's white BMW pull up in front of her house. She got up from the sofa to open the door and let her in. As soon as she saw Pam's face she began to cry. Without saying a word Pam reached out and hugged Diamond. After closing the door the two women walked into the living room where Diamond returned to her seat on the sofa.

"Can I get you anything to drink?" Diamond asked, trying to look past her mental state and play the perfect hostess.

"No, I'm fine, baby. When you called I came right over. What's going on? You know I hate to see you cry, makes me want to cry and I absolutely hate messing up my makeup." She laughed, trying to lighten up Diamond's mood.

"I'm just so stressed right now. Nothing is going right for me. I thought that Black and me had a relationship that was unbreakable but now I'm realizing that what we have isn't much different than any other relationship," Diamond replied.

"What's the problem though? I mean is there anything that you can think of that may have caused a distance?"

"No. I mean a month ago we were fine then all of a sudden things changed. I know in my heart that he's cheating one me. I stood outside the room and heard him talking to a woman on the phone. Then he hasn't been coming home every night."

"So you know for a fact that he was talking to a woman?" Pam asked, trying to figure out where things went wrong.

"I mean no, I don't have concrete proof. I wasn't on the line but I can tell by the way that he was talking that he wasn't talking to a man. I just don't know what it is that I did to make him feel like he needs to cheat. It makes me think about the time that he cheated with Trice. You know I had to intentionally get pregnant to keep him?" Diamond blurted by mistake. Besides Kiki, she'd never told anyone that she purposely got pregnant.

"So in other words you trapped him? Did you ever think that he might have found out?"

"No, I don't think that he's found out and even if he did I don't think that would be a reason to cheat." She paused.

"Well, men don't always have the best reasons to cheat but they don't think with their brains at those times either."

"I just need to figure out what's going on because right now I'm so lost. At least if I knew what he was upset about I could work on fixing it but right now he won't tell me anything."

"Sometimes men will shut you out, but if you truly want to be with him and keep your family together you can't give up. There were times that I thought my family was being torn apart. You know I've been on both sides of the fence, the mistress and the wife, so I know how it feels. I never expected my relationship with your father to be all peaches and cream because of the way that it started. Nothing that starts out that way goes on without a few bumps in the road. It all takes work whether good or bad," Pam said, rubbing Diamond's arm, trying to console her.

"So do you think I should approach her?"

"No, I think that you should approach him," Pam quickly replied.

"I've tried to confront him but all he does is push me away."

"Well, you have to keep trying. I know I didn't raise you, Diamond, but I didn't birth any children who are wimps. I have fighter genes and I know that you have it in you."

"You're right, I am a fighter. I'm not going to give up on my family just yet. I worked too hard to have it to just let someone come in and steal it all away. Thanks for being here for me. I truly appreciate all that you've done for me."

"You don't have to thank me, you're my daughter and I love you too much to just allow you to cry without a shoulder to lean on. You can always call me when you need me," Pam said with a smile.

Diamond extended her arms to hug Pam. The conversation with Pam was just the push that she needed. Pam stayed for a few more moments before leaving. Diamond immediately picked up her phone and called Black.

After the phone rang a few times, Black answered, immediately letting out a sigh before speaking. "Yeah."

"Are you coming home today? I really want to sit down and talk. I don't like the way that we are right now. Black, it's killing me."

"Yeah, I will be home later, Diamond," he replied in a lighter tone.

"Okay, I will see you then."

"All right," he said before ending the call.

She smiled, as he didn't give her the usual brush-off response that she was expecting. His reaction made her feel as if things weren't done and there was a strong chance for reconciliation.

She headed upstairs to her room and took a shower before patiently waiting for Black to arrive. She'd fallen asleep waiting for the time to pass and was awakened by a tap on her foot and a whisper of her name.

"Hey, I fell asleep waiting," she said as she rubbed her eyes to get a clear view of him. He was standing at the bottom of the bed.

"Did you still want to talk?" he asked before sitting down on the edge of the bed.

"I'm just trying to figure out what's going on with us. I feel like we're falling apart, Black, and I don't want to lose you," she said as she scooted to the edge of the bed to sit next to him. "Is it something that I did? I mean if so, let me know and I will fix it."

"It's not you, Diamond. I just have a lot of shit on my mind. I'm trying to straighten out all of this shit that's going on in the street and keep you happy at the same time. It's hard, Diamond, because you have a tendency to over think things and push when it isn't necessary."

"I only act that way because I care, Black. I love you too much to lose you."

"You just gotta give me a little breathing room, Diamond. I don't need you on my back all the time like my mother. I need a wife. I need the wife I fell in love with."

"So what are you asking me to do, Black?"

"I don't know, Diamond. I'm just tired of the bickering and arguing for nothing. It used to be fun coming home, now I almost dread it." He spoke sharply.

Diamond sat silent for a few minutes, thinking about what he'd just said to her. She never wanted him to dread coming home and it was never her intention to make him unhappy. She wanted to ask him about the phone call but she was afraid he'd cut the conversation short. "Black, I understand how you feel completely and I'm sorry, okay? I just want things to go back to the way that they were," she pleaded as she placed her hand on top of his right hand, which was resting on his thigh. "Please, Black, I need you," she said softly as she grabbed his chin to turn his face toward her. Without allowing him to respond she kissed him.

He grabbed her around her waist and pushed her back onto the bed. All of his emotions rushed to the surface of his skin as if they'd never left. There wasn't any doubt that he loved her, but as a man he struggled with his thirst for other women. He lay on top of her and caressed every inch of her skin, which was revealed. Her skin was soft as cotton and carried the scent of Victoria's Secret Love Spell. Soon, his kisses moved from her lips to her neck and from her neck to her breasts, which were protruding from the center of her black lace bra. After treating them with equal attention he moved down to her belly button, slowly sticking his tongue in and out of the center. Every so often she'd let out a moan as she fought to hold in the evidence of ecstasy. With one hand he pulled her panties down as she lifted up a little to allow an easy removal. With her pussy fully exposed he didn't waste any time burying his face in between her legs and sticking his thick tongue into her moist opening. With all the energy that she had bottle up just the slightest tickle nearly caused an orgasm.

"Oh shit," she moaned as he slid the middle and index fingers of his right hand inside of her. She began to sway her hips as he pulled his fingers in and out while using his tongue to focus on her clit.

Black remained silent as his dick was growing more and more by the second. With her moans providing the soundtrack and the sensitivity of his stiff dick, he was fighting to hold in his own eruption. He was positioned in front of the bed on his knees with her legs folding over his shoulders. After a few more minutes of fondling her G-spot he felt the rush of her juices on his fingertips run down to the palm of his hand. Her body shook uncontrollably as her legs briefly tightened around his head, firmly holding him in place. Her release was his cue and he simultaneously unzipped his pants, slid his boxers down, and thrust his long dick deep inside of her. Her body immediately tensed up as he placed both of his hands under the arch in her back on both sides. Getting a rhythm going he picked up speed, filling her walls completely. He looked down at her as she stared at him, biting her lower lip. The small beads of sweat that formed on different areas of her face illuminated her beauty. She was just as stunning if not more so as the day he'd met her. She could tell by the look on his face that even in this moment of passion he was deep in thought.

"I love you," Black blurted as he continued to move in and out of her. It was at that moment that he felt sorry for all that he'd done and made a decision to do his best to make things right between them. He continued to force himself as far as he could go before leaning down to kiss her. She stuck her tongue through his lips and began to massage his tongue. Knowing that he was nearing his peak she wrapped her arms around his back and held him tightly. After a few more thrusts every ounce of his cum was flowing out of him, inside of her, and then out on the bed, forming a small puddle underneath her. The two lay connected without saying a word for the next five minutes before he pulled himself from inside of her, gasping for air as the sensitivity of his semi-hard dick almost erupted again.

He got up and gathered his clothing from the floor while she still lay on the edge of the bed not sure of what to say. Knowing their lovemaking session wouldn't solve all of their problems, it was a start. She could hear the shower come on in the bathroom and immediately she assumed that he would be right back on his way out. Surprisingly, after he was done showering and she followed him, he was asleep on his side of the bed when she reentered the room. Quietly, she climbed into bed, moved near him, and wrapped her arm around him.

Chapter Twelve

Mr. Perfect?

"What do you mean you're quitting?" Lucky's best friend and confidant Alisha asked, concerned that she was making too drastic of a decision.

"I mean exactly what I just said, I'm quitting and I'm moving in with him," Lucky said as she folded articles of clothing and stuffed them into suitcases and bags that were lying open on her bed.

"Why are you rushing, Lucky? You just met him. How could you possibly know that much about him to be comfortable enough with quitting your job and moving in with him? What about your tuition? I mean is he going to pay that? I would hate to see you mess up school. You've come too far for that."

"I know how far I've come, Alisha, and obviously I wouldn't let anyone mess up my education. You of all people know how important that is to me. He knows how important that is to me, Lish. I know that you don't know him at all but give him a chance. He's a good man. I feel it in my heart and usually my heart doesn't steer me wrong, even when my body and mind try to. Come on, you've always been supportive and I still need you. Don't back out on me now regardless of how foolish the decision may seem. The reality of the situation is, if things don't go as planned, which I'm not going to even think that way, but if for some reason that happens, I'm going to still need you to have my back."

Alisha sat there shaking her head, feeling like her friend was making the biggest mistake of her life, but she knew that once her mind was made up it was almost impossible to change it. She also knew to continue to try could ultimately cause damage to their friendship, so she realized that sitting back and being supportive was the best thing that she could do.

"So when do I meet Mr. Perfect?" she said, breaking the ice. "I mean I need to at least meet the man before he steals my best friend away." She laughed, trying to make light of the situation, although deep down she wasn't happy at all.

She was still worried. She remembered the last time Lucky had made a swift decision like this with a man that almost ended her life. His name was Jeff, Jeff Pearson, and she was head over heels in love with him quickly. The two met after a basketball game and kept constant contact but immediately what Lucky saw as love Alisha saw as insecurity, and slowly but surely his true colors shined through. It wasn't long before Lucky became pregnant with his child, which Alisha swore was all in his plan to begin with. Leave it up to Jeff the condom broke by accident, but Alisha truly believed that he poked holes inside of the condoms to ensure that she'd bear his seed.

To make matters even worse, he became abusive, and there were many nights the two were sitting in the ER nursing a busted lip or a bruised body part. Regardless, Alisha was there by her side and she always tried to encourage her and support her decisions, despite how foolish they were. Ultimately, the beatings led to a miscarriage, and even though that was the saddest that she'd ever seen her friend, she realized it was probably the best thing that could have happened to her. The loss of the child was just the thing to force Jeff to walk away, and though it devastated Lucky and would take months to get her back on track, she had been the best that she'd ever seen her since then. So she wasn't selfish at all; she was worried that she would end up seeing a replay of 2007: the year of hell, as she called it.

After a few moments of hesitation Lucky responded to her question. She wasn't all that eager to introduce her to Reed because she wasn't always very optimistic when it came to her relationships. For one, she never believed that she was good at choosing the right man, but she never thought that anyone she didn't personally handpick herself was the right one for that matter. She was always nervous when it came time for an introduction. She let out a sigh and finally replied, "Soon enough, you will meet him. And why do you have to call him Mr. Perfect? Don't start, Alisha, okay?" She pointed toward her friend with a bit of sassiness.

"Okay, okay. It was just a joke, Lucky. I get it, you're in love, and I'm happy for you, don't get me wrong. But I love you and you know I don't want to see you hurt. You know I'd kill a nigga over you." She laughed but was dead serious.

"I know and I appreciate it, but you can't breastfeed a baby forever. At some point you gotta snatch the titty away!" She grabbed her breast and made a popping sound.

Alisha mugged her and knocked her onto the bed and both women burst into laughter. There wasn't anything that could break these two apart and there had been plenty of people, things, and situations that had tried.

"Can we stop all this packing and shit for a minute? I need a drink, girl, a real one!" Alisha blurted, getting up from the bed.

Lucky rose from the bed and threw the handful of clothing she had in her hand down onto the suitcase. "Sure, I can use a drink myself."

"Okay, then, let's go."

The two gathered their things and headed toward the door to go to the corner bar to get a few drinks. Alisha exited before Lucky, who was locking the door when a white Porsche pulled up in front of the door. Both women looked at each other, unsure of who the driver was. The windows were darkened so they couldn't see who was inside until the car's ignition turned off and the driver exited. A woman dressed expensively from head to toe headed straight for Lucky and Alisha. Lucky looked the woman up and down as she removed her sunglasses before speaking.

"I'm looking for a woman named Lucky," Raquel spoke in an assertive tone.

"I'm Lucky, how can I help you?" Lucky stepped forward, making sure the woman knew she wasn't intimidated.

"How are you doing?" She extended her hand to shake Lucky's hand. "My name is Raquel. I'm married to Chance, the guy you're currently seeing."

Lucky looked confused.

"Oh, Reed, sorry. I guess that's the name you know him by. Chancellor Reed is his full name, in case you didn't know. Well, I'm his wife. I'm sure he told you he was married but I'm not here to rain on your parade not one bit. I'm here because I've moved on totally and the problem is he's contesting the divorce. I figured, if he had a new relationship and all what's the point of holding on to the past you know? I'm just here to see if you can talk to him to speed things up, because I have a man who's waiting to marry me and I can't do that until he signs those papers you know." She giggled.

Lucky stood there stone-faced. She was certain this woman had other motives for finding out where she lived and approaching her besides some fucking divorce papers. "Okay, so excuse me if I'm confused here. You really came all the way to my home to tell me that Reed, excuse me, I mean *Chancellor Reed* won't sign divorce papers?"

"That's exactly what I'm telling you, hun. Listen, I don't want him and I certainly don't want to impede your relationship with him. Honestly, I'm ecstatic that he was able to come home and find somebody to love because I was done with him a long time ago. I just want him off of my back that's all. I came here on some woman-to-woman shit hoping you could see where I was coming from."

"Actually I don't see where you're coming from . . . uhhh what's your name again?"

"Raquel. Raquel Reed."

"Okay, well, Mrs. Raquel Reed. I will make sure that I pass the message along to him but that's all that I can promise you."

"And that's all that I ask. I appreciate your assistance, Lucky. You ladies have a good evening." She placed her shades back on and walked back to her car.

Both Lucky and Alisha stood there staring at her car until she pulled off and turned the corner. Alisha immediately looked at Lucky and spoke. "Really? Was she fucking serious?"

"The sad part is I think she was," Lucky responded, shaking her head.

"Well what are you gonna do?"

"I don't know, do you think I should call him? I mean I don't even know how I should feel about it. She wasn't really disrespectful."

"Oh the bitch was disrespectful by coming to your house, that shit was out of fucking line, Lucky. Seriously. I tried to fall back but you know me, the ghetto was about to come out. I wanted to punch that bitch in her face!" Alisha yelled.

"You know I'm not immediately hostile, Lish."

"Well, you should be, that shit was crazy. I would be calling his ass right now snapping the fuck out. I mean really, is this what you have to look forward to? Ex-wives—I mean *wives*—showing up at your door and shit," Alisha said, pacing back and forth. "Shit if I could use a drink before I *really* need one now."

"Well, let's go get a drink so you can calm down then because I'm calm. I'm not going to let her ruin my evening. I will discuss it with him later." Her cell phone began to ring and caught both of them off guard. It was Reed. "It's him," she said, looking at Alisha to figure out what to do.

"Well, answer it," Alisha said, motioning with her hands.

For some reason she was nervous about picking up the phone. It was almost as if her fairy tale had somehow been tarnished. She knew about his wife but she was hoping that everything he'd told her from the beginning was true. She wanted so much to believe in him. The last thing that she wanted was for Alisha to see their relationship at odds, especially after she'd made him seem like Prince Charming. So she wasn't sure if it was a good time to have the inevitable conversation regarding Raquel, but she didn't want to ignore his call either.

"Hello," she said in an unruffled tone.

"Hey, babe. Did Raquel just stop by your house?"

"Yes. Actually she just left, how did you know?" she asked.

"I'm so sorry about that, babe. She called my phone laughing about how she'd spoken to you. Are you still home?"

"I'm outside of my house on my way to get a drink with my friend Alisha."

"Are you still moving some of your things over tonight?"

"Yes," she replied without hesitation.

"Okay, well call me when you're done with your friend and I will come by to pick you up. I have some things to talk to you about."

"Okay, I will call you when I'm done," she said before ending the call.

"Well what did he say?" Alisha asked anxiously.

"He asked me if she had come by here and we would talk later on when I'm done with you."

"That's it?" Alisha asked with one hand on her hip.

"What do you mean *that's it?* Girl, you are a mess! Let's go to the bar please and pick this conversation up another day," Lucky said, nudging Alisha on her shoulder off of the steps.

"I'll drop it for now." She laughed.

The two women headed to the bar and had their drinks without incident. They managed to have girl talk without Reed or Raquel being the topic of conversation. The two hung out at the bar for two hours before walking back to Lucky's house and parting ways. Lucky obediently called Reed to let him know that she was home, and soon he would be arriving to pick her up.

She was packed and ready when he rang the bell. She opened the door with a smile as he stood looking as delicious as well-done steak.

"Is this all you're bringing?" he asked, looking down at the small suitcase she had with her.

"For now." She smiled. "You look yummy." She leaned in to kiss him. "What, you have a date or something?"

"As a matter of fact I do. I have a date with your backside. I'm gonna hit it all night long." He laughed.

"Is that right?"

"Oh yeah," he said, tapping her from behind as she walked toward the car.

She quietly got inside and waited for him to get in. She wasn't about to be the one to bring up Raquel; she was waiting for him to say what it was he needed to say about it. The whole situation was pretty awkward for Lucky. She'd never dealt with a man who was married, and even though he was in the process of a divorce, legally, he was still married.

Reed closed the trunk and climbed into the car and rubbed the back of her hand. Inside, he was dreading having the "Raquel conversation." He was angry and frustrated but he didn't want her to think that things were out of his control. He'd quickly fallen for Lucky and he wasn't about to let his past ruin his future. He'd been honest with Lucky about his relationship with her and he hated the fact that she was attempting to put doubt in her mind.

"So what did Raquel say to you?"

"She said that she served you with divorce papers and you have yet to sign them. I mean I thought you wanted a divorce, Reed?"

"It's much more complicated than that. Trust me, I don't want anything more than to be divorced from her, believe me. I have been honest

with you about my situation with her from day
one. I have not lied to you. The reason that I
haven't signed the papers is because she's trying
to get half of everything that I own and I refuse
to let that scandalous woman do that to me. She's
taken so much from me and she's still trying to
take like a fucking leech. You know she hasn't
done shit for my daughter. She doesn't even call
her, it's like she doesn't even exist. All she wants
is money."

Lucky sat attentive, taking in everything that
he said. She wanted to make sure that she didn't
miss anything, to avoid the deer-in-headlights
look that she displayed when Raquel approached
her earlier that day.

"I want you to trust me. I would never ask you
to quit your job and leave your comfort zone if I
was on some bullshit. I'm through with her. I'm
just trying to protect what's mine, you feel me?"
He grabbed hold of her hand and looked her in
the eye.

She felt a sigh of relief. Hearing him say that
he was finished with her was the confirmation
that she needed. He fairy tale was still a fairy tale
and he was still Mr. Perfect.

"Do you still trust me?"

Without any hesitation she replied, "Yes, I still
trust you. It's gonna take a lot more than that to
get rid of me."

"Well, I'm glad to hear that, 'cause I was worried for a second when you came out with one bag. I know you have way more shit than that."

"I wanted to scare you a little bit." She laughed.

He laughed with her and turned on the ignition. Both of them felt much more relaxed then they had before. Reed was even more determined to deal with his situation with Raquel as quickly as possible before she ruined his life any more than she already had.

After reaching his house he reluctantly told Lucky that he had to make a run once he received a phone call on his cell phone that he took in the other room.

"I promise, I'll be back before you know it." Reed spoke before kissing her on the forehead.

"I guess I need to get used to it if I'm going to be living here, right?" She smiled.

"Sure, you're right," he replied, smiling from ear to ear. With that he kissed her on the forehead once more before heading out of the house and jumping into his car.

Soon, she heard the loud boom of his car radio and his car speeding down the street.

Chapter Thirteen

Open Season

Click, Click . . . Even in her sleep, the sound was all too familiar. It was a sound that almost ruined her life. The sound that altered the path that her life would take and every twist and turn that would follow. Because she knew what followed the sound, she was afraid to open her eyes.

She lay there in bed, still hoping that the noise was only part of a horrible dream. Instead she opened her eyes to face the barrel of a 9 mm handgun.

"Don't scream, don't speak, or I'll blow your muthafucking brains out, bitch!" The deep tone boomed through the black ski mask that accompanied the all-black attire the stranger wore.

Tears instantly began to fall from Diamond's eyes. She kept her weeping silent as he slowly pulled her from the bed and dragged her down the long hall that led to the stairs. She wondered where the hell Black was as flashbacks of the day she murdered Kemp came to mind. She could clearly see his lifeless body falling to the floor as if it had just happened yesterday. She tried to focus and obey his commands as they headed down the stairs, but she needed to know if Black was okay.

"Where is my husband?" she asked in a low tone.

Without a response, he used the butt of the gun to hit her in the back of the head. The hard steel instantly sent her tumbling down the stairs. She hit almost every step before reaching the bottom, where she cried in agony. She couldn't move but she could hear his footsteps nearing the spot where she was lying.

"Learn how to follow directions! You'd think a fine bitch like you would have the brains for this, especially a bitch who likes to murder niggas." He laughed.

How the hell did he know that? she thought as she continued to lie in pain on the cold cherry-wood floor. She knew that he would have to know her personally to know what she'd done. She wished that she could rip off the mask that he wore to find out who he was, but out of fear she tried to relax.

"Get the fuck up!" he yelled.

She struggled to get up from the floor but every part of her body ached from the fall. After realizing that she might not be able to stand alone, he grabbed her by the arm tightly and pulled her up. They headed toward the dining room where Black was seated at the head of the table, tied up. There was duct tape across his mouth and blood running down both sides of his face.

"Oh my God, baby, are you okay?" She tried to run over to him but the guy who had been leading her into the room wrapped his arm around her neck and pulled her back to the other end of the table. He pushed her down into the chair as she rubbed her neck. It was at that point she realized that they really meant business. Not that she didn't believe it when they pulled her out of bed, but deep down she hoped that it was all a dream. She knew now that it wasn't and she was wide awake and in pain all over. She said a silent prayer for them to make it out of this alive. Black was sitting there with blood all over his face and shirt. They had really done a number on him. She wanted to just get it over with and give them whatever it was that they wanted so that she could get back to her life.

"What did you do to him?" she asked as he forced her into the chair that was near where she was standing. The man hit her on the back of the head again. It was still throbbing in pain from the hit she'd received a few minutes back.

"Yo, I'm going to kill this bitch in a minute. She won't shut the fuck up!" he yelled to his partner as he began pacing back and forth behind her.

"Calm down," yelled the taller, leaner guy who stood near Black.

Black sat there, looking at her, shaking his head. She figured he was most likely trying to tell her to obey their commands but she couldn't. She couldn't just sit there not knowing what the hell it was they wanted from her. If she was going to die she was at least going to know why. She'd never been one to go down without a fight and she wasn't about to start now. Her mind was all over the place. She was looking around the room to see if there was any way that she could get them out of there.

"Please tell me what you want," she cried. They all began laughing as if she'd told a hilarious joke. She didn't see what the hell was so funny.

"Look, bitch, common sense would tell you we ain't drop in to say hi. We know that you stashed up some money when you left the game and we're here to collect."

"We don't have a lot of money. Most of it is tied up in real estate."

"She just doesn't get it, I see," the taller one yelled before punching her on the right side of her face.

She felt like he'd broken her jaw instantly. Blood was now running out of her mouth.

"Now we're going to try this shit again. We know you have that money. Y'all living in this big-ass house, driving these fly-ass cars, jewels and shit. Bitch, I wasn't born yesterday. We want five hundred thousand dollars by Friday."

"Friday? You can't be serious, there's no way I can get that to you by Friday."

"Does it look like we're laughing?" The armed guy behind her bent down and yelled into her ear, "Hell, those cars you drive, you might want get rid of those, that's a start."

"And what if I can't come up with it?" she asked.

"You really wanna see how serious I am?" Without flinching, the man who was standing near Black raised his gun and shot Black in the head at point-blank range. Blood and brain matter covered the ivory-colored walls. Black's body slumped over and blood poured from the gaping wound in his head.

Diamond screamed so loud it echoed throughout the house and probably throughout the neighborhood. She pulled away from the grips of her captor, who didn't try to hold on to her.

He was shocked himself and currently yelling at the gunman for shooting Black. "What the fuck are you doing?" He stormed over toward the gunman, who raised the gun in his direction.

"Yo, back the fuck up, nigga, and control this bitch before I shoot her ass too."

Diamond was kneeling next to Black's lifeless body and cradling his face in her hands, which were both covered with blood.

"Get that fucking gun out of my face." The two men were now standing face to face as Diamond wept below them. The gunman backed down, then proceeded to pick Diamond up from the floor himself and pushed her across the room.

She slammed into the wall, causing a loud thump. She immediately bounced off of the wall and fell to the floor. Her body was racked with pain and sorrow. After all that she'd done and all that she'd been through she never imagined that things would turn out this way. Though she'd done a lot of wrong to a lot of people she always hoped that the good that she'd done would somehow outweigh the bad. As she lay there with her face buried in the hardwood floor, tears seeped into the cracks. She was shaking uncontrollably as visions of Black's brain being splattered across the room played in her mind.

The other man was now standing near Diamond and looking across the room at the gunman who was visibly annoyed. He was frustrated, as the evening's events weren't going as planned and the gunman appeared to have plans of his own. Not only was he part of a robbery; he was now a part of murder.

"Can we wrap this shit up?" he yelled, directing his speech at the gunman.

"Certainly, get her ass up off the ground." He pointed at Diamond.

The taller masked man picked Diamond up off the ground and moved her over to the chair. She closed her eyes to avoid seeing Black. The gunman made his way over to the end of the table where she was seated and stood in front of her. He wanted to make sure that she was clear on what they needed and when then they needed it.

"Now, what is it that we need and when do we need it?" he asked as he bent down in front of her and grabbed her chin, forcing her to look him in the eye.

"Five hundred thousand dollars by Friday."

"Good girl," he said, patting her on the top of her head with the tip of his gun. "Now just in case you're thinking about doing something stupid, we have some insurance. Your little girl—"

Diamond jumped out of her chair to attack him and was immediately knocked back down by the gun-toting masked man.

"Don't do it. If you ever want to see her again you'll calm the fuck down."

Diamond sat in the chair, sobbing. She'd just lost her husband and now faced losing her only child as well. It was all too much to handle and she didn't care about living without them.

"Your little girl will be returned safely once we get our money."

"How will I find you?"

"You won't. We'll find you, and if you have all of the money, we will return your daughter as promised."

"And what if I can't get the money?" she asked honestly, as she didn't know where or how she was going to get $500,000 on such short notice.

"Well, then you can kiss your little girl good-bye. I'd hate to be a child killer so I know you're going to do everything in your power to get the money to us."

"Can I just see her? Please, I just want to make sure that she's okay. Where did you take her?"

"She's safe, don't worry about that. I'd like to think I'm a man of my word and I'd also like to think that you're a woman of yours. So as long as those statements are true then neither of us has anything to worry about."

Diamond continued to plead with him to allow her to see Dior. Without Black, she was the most important thing in the world. Her mind was spinning and the physical pain that she'd felt before was now masked by adrenaline. She knew that she had to do whatever it took. Even if she had to rob, steal, or commit another murder she would if it meant she would get her daughter back in her arms. Her survival instincts kicked in and suddenly her tears dried up and tremors ceased. Without even the slightest tremble in her voice she spoke, "Okay, so what am I supposed to tell the cops about his body?"

The masked men looked at her, then looked at each other before the leader of the pack spoke. "Tell them exactly what happened, three niggas broke in your house, shot him, whipped your ass, and kidnapped your daughter for ransom."

"And then what? If I tell them she's been taken for ransom they'll be on me like flies to shit. I'll never be able to get the money together with them on my back."

"You're a smart girl, Diamond, you got away with murder. I'm sure you can figure this shit out. This should be as easy as taking candy from a baby."

Diamond stood there deep in thought. He was right—she'd gotten away with murder before and if she made it through this shit alive she was damn sure going to try to get away with it again. There was no way that she was going to let them breathe after what they'd put her through. She kept a stone face as the other two men headed toward the door and the leader of the group looked her in the eye and gave her a smirk before extending his hand to shake hers. She looked down at his hand as if it were diseased, but she knew that she needed to play along to avoid pissing him off.

"Pleasure doing business with you," he said while firmly gripping her hand. He pulled her close enough to whisper in her ear. "Just remember what I said and you'll be fine." He released her hand and followed the other two men out of the door.

As soon as the door shut she slid down to the floor and began to sob once more. She stared at Black and began to apologize to him. She blamed herself for everything, thinking that this was all somehow tied to Kemp's murder.

Again, she thought, *it's all coming back to bite me in the ass.* The pain from all of the punches that she'd sustained was now coming back with a vengeance. Her body was stiffening as she attempted to get up from the floor to crawl over to the phone to call 911. She dreaded speaking to the police about the night's events because she would have to twist the truth in an attempt to save her daughter's life. She took a deep breath before dialing; within a few seconds the female operator's voice came through the receiver.

"Nine-one-one, what's your emergency?"

"I need an ambulance and the police, my husband's been shot. I've been beaten and my daughter's been kidnapped. Please send help, please hurry." She dropped the phone to the floor. In the distance she could hear the operator through the receiver.

"Ma'am, are you there? Ma'am, if you're there please pick up the phone."

Diamond sat with her back against the wall with tears streaming down her face as she waited for the police and ambulance to arrive. As her husband lay dead less than four feet away from her, she watched the clock ticking on the wall, knowing that every minute counted. Every minute that passed was a minute wasted, and by the looks of things, she didn't have any minutes to spare.

The police were the first to arrive and the ambulance arrived moments later. Black was pronounced dead at the scene and Diamond refused medical treatment each time it was offered.

"Ma'am, you really need medical treatment. Your jaw could possibly be broken and you could have internal bleeding from some of the blows that you sustained," the male technician pleaded with Diamond, but his case was sadly falling on deaf ears.

"What part of no don't you understand? I already told you that I'm not going to the hospital. My child is missing and I need to do everything that I can to find her. Sitting up in a hospital just won't do," she yelled. "Now could you please hurry up and wrap up these cuts because I really need to get out and look for my child."

Black's body had since been taken out of the house by the medical examiner and different sections of the house were now taped off with yellow police tape. It almost resembled something that you'd only see on TV. There was a large pool of blood on the floor under where Black had slumped off the chair and there were remnants of his brain matter splattered all over the walls and other surfaces. Her home was filled with detectives and other crime scene personnel.

Outside, there was a huge crowd forming as the tenants of the high-class cul-de-sac weren't used to such a large police presence, and they most definitely weren't used to home invasions and children being taken for ransom. The news vans from channels three, six, ten, seventeen, and twenty-nine were parked outside of their house as well. The spectacle was all too much for Diamond as she was becoming more frustrated by the second, but she continued to try to hold it together to evade any suspicion.

"How long is this going to take? I really need to make some calls."

"I'll be done in a few minutes, please just bear with me," the technician said as he shook his head and mumbled under his breath. He was a father so he knew that, put in her position, he'd probably feel the same way, but he also knew that there was a proper way to handle every situation and it was his opinion that she was going about things totally wrong.

Diamond, on the other hand, believed that she was doing what was right and that there wasn't any other way to handle a situation like this one.

"Okay, all done. Now, make sure you come in to the hospital tomorrow to get these two stitched up. If not, you'll risk infection and the scars will take a lot longer to heal."

"Okay, got it, now are you done?" she asked with sarcasm. Immediately she got up from the chair, grabbed her purse, and headed toward the door.

"You can't leave, Mrs. Black. You have to be around in case the kidnappers call," the lead detective spoke, catching Diamond heading out of the door.

"Last time I checked I wasn't a child, you weren't my mother, and I wasn't under arrest. So unless you plan on shooting or arresting me, I'm leaving. I have to find my child."

"No, you're not under arrest, yet, but you can be for obstruction of justice. We still need to go over the rest of the details of the events that led you here, and we also need to talk to you about any enemies your husband might have had, or anything that may be useful in our search for your daughter as well as your husband's killer. I know it's tough and I can't imagine what you're going through, but your husband would want you to do this right. I'm sure he wouldn't want it any other way," the female detective spoke, attempting to place her hand on Diamond's shoulder.

Diamond quickly snatched her arm away from her. "First off, you don't know shit about my husband and you damn sure don't know shit about me, so you can't begin to tell me what he would've wanted. Now again, if I'm not under arrest I really have to go." Diamond looked the detective up and down, waiting for her response.

"Well, if you want to do this the hard way so be it. Officers, arrest her please for obstruction of justice." She flagged the two uniformed officers in their direction.

"What? No, you can't do that," Diamond yelled, causing a scene.

The spectators outside of the house looked on in confusion.

"Cuff her," the detective instructed.

"Please, you can't do this," Diamond screamed, trying to pull away from the officer's grip.

"You have the right to remain silent. Anything you say can be held against you in a court of law. You have the right to an attorney. If you cannot afford an attorney, one will be provided to you free of charge. Do you understand these rights as they have been read to you?" The female detective read her Miranda rights clearly and distinctively.

"Please, my daughter will die if you do this. Please don't arrest me." Diamond began to cry as her temper had just written her a check that her ass couldn't cash.

"Do you understand these rights as they have been read to you?" she repeated.

"Yes, I understand, but please don't take me to jail. I need to be home to find my baby." She pleaded as tears were pouring from her eyes.

The female detective stood looking at her, wanting to stop her from being taken away, but knowing that she had a duty to find out who was guilty of the bloodshed that had taken place that evening. She watched Diamond sob as the officers escorted her out of the house, placed her in the back of the car, and shut the door. She had no intention of keeping her in prison more than she needed to; however, if she refused to cooperate she wouldn't have a choice. The detective looked over at her partner, who stood behind her just as confused as she was.

Shaking his head he spoke, "There's definitely more to this than meets the eye."

"Oh, I'm sure of that."

Both of them reentered the house to wrap up before heading down to the station.

Diamond rode in the back of the police car with many thoughts running through her mind. She silently prayed that things would work out for her. The sooner that she could be released from their custody, the better. *How did things get so out of control?* she thought. Just a few hours earlier she was looking forward to getting her relationship with Black back on track. Now as she rode in the back of the police cruiser it was evident that nothing in her life would be the same or even resemble anything from the past. The man she thought she would spend the rest of her life with had been stripped away. It was almost as if her heart had been ripped out of her chest and stomped into a million little pieces. Realizing that crying wouldn't save her daughter, she knew what she had to do. After her last tear fell, she gently placed her head on the back of the seat and closed her eyes.

Chapter Fourteen

The Ties That Bind

"You waited up for me?" Reed asked, entering the bedroom and noticing Lucky sitting up at the head of the bed watching an episode of *CSI: Miami.*

"Of course I did. I wanted to make sure that my man made it in safely." She smiled.

"Well, I need you to wait up just a little bit more. I want to jump in the shower. I've been out running the streets all day." He smiled while leaning on the bed to kiss her.

"Yeah, that would be a good idea. You definitely smell like you've been *outside* all day." She laughed.

He playfully pushed her shoulder, making her fall onto the bed. "It's cool, a nigga knows when he stinks." He laughed while heading to the bathroom. Once inside the bathroom he quickly removed his clothes and placed them inside of the trash bag and tied the bag in a knot before tucking it under the bathroom sink. After turning on the shower he looked at himself in the mirror.

"What have I gotten myself into?" he said while shaking his head. Things hadn't gone as planned and now he wasn't sure what move he should make next. He tried to keep the situation a secret from Romeo but after Justice put a gun to his chest he realized that Brook might not be his only enemy.

He got in the shower and stood under the hot water, hoping to rinse away all of his sins and any remnant of blood that may have been left behind. After leaving the shower and going back into the bedroom he kept as quiet as possible, noticing Lucky sound asleep. Instead of waking her and creating dialogue that he wasn't ready for, he climbed into bed, avoiding any physical contact that might disturb her peaceful sleep. With one hand behind his head and the other across his chest, he stared at the ceiling, replaying Justice calmly pulling the trigger and killing Black. Though he'd witnessed many murders, he'd never witnessed one that, in his heart, he believed was unjust. He couldn't for the life of him figure out why Black needed to die or why the hell their daughter needed to be taken. So many decisions appeared to have been made without thinking about what effect it could have had on his life. It was almost as if all of his plans for getting his own life straightened out had taken a back seat to what Johnny wanted. The more he thought about it the more he wished that he'd never agreed to get involved in the first place. He had to figure out a way out of it before it damaged his life and any plan that he had for himself. Realizing how exhausted he truly was, he allowed his body to relax, and soon he was drifting off to sleep.

The following morning he woke up to the smell of bacon and, after looking over to his right at the empty space that was occupied by Lucky the night before, he smiled. He loved a woman who catered to her man. He immediately thought about Raquel and how she used to do things to satisfy him until she got the ring on her finger and things quickly changed. She was more interested in designer clothes and handbags than making him happy, and eventually he began to feel the same way. He'd been raised to honor and respect his wife, and he tried his best to be the man his mother would have wanted him to be. He was enjoying his time with Lucky, but naturally he wondered if he was taking things too fast. He hadn't even gotten his divorce and the last thing that he wanted to do was hurt Lucky. Raquel was unpredictable so he had to make sure to be prepared for anything that she threw his way.

He got out of bed, and after brushing his teeth he joined her in the kitchen, where she had a plate ready with a tall glass of orange juice on the side. Looking even more delicious then the feast that she had prepared, Lucky stood naked with only an apron covering her curvy frame. He'd have to resist the temptation to jump her bones and make it through breakfast. He leaned on the frame of the kitchen doorway, looking her up and down while licking his lips.

"I thought I was gonna have to come drag you out of bed." She laughed, walking over to him and kissing him on the lips. "Come on and see what I made for you," she said, grabbing him by the arm and dragging him over to the island where the meal awaited him.

"This looks good, baby. I can't believe that you did all of this for me." He smiled.

"I don't know why not, you know you're my boo." She laughed.

"Well are you going to join me? I only see one plate here," he said, sitting down on the high stool.

"No, I'm not a big breakfast eater. Besides, I'd rather stand here and admire you enjoying all of my hard work." She walked around to the opposite side of the island and leaned her elbows on the countertop.

"Well, then it's probably best that you stay on that side of the counter or I won't be dining on this food for damn sure." He laughed.

"Why, is my outfit that irresistible?" she asked, standing straight up and turning in a circle to give him a full view of the lack of clothing she was wearing.

"You knew exactly what you were doing when you put that shit on, but it's cool. I'm going to eat this good food here, and then I'm gonna eat that good pussy, so I hope you're prepared for it 'cause I'm gonna get busy, you hear me?" He laughed as he bowed his head to say a silent prayer before grabbing his fork and practically swallowing the food without chewing.

Lucky stood on the opposite side of the island, laughing so hard that tears were quickly forming in her eyes. "Don't choke. I'm not CPR certified." She continued to chuckle.

"Oh, I can eat very well. I'm definitely not going to choke, so you don't have to even worry about that." He smiled before taking a bite of his bacon.

"Oh, I know you can *eat*." She smiled, getting a slight chill just thinking about the things that he could do with his lips and tongue. He was certainly blessed by the best in the lovemaking department.

It took Reed all of five minutes to demolish his food, and after going over to the sink to rinse his mouth of excess food, he turned around, ready to pay extra special attention to his woman. When he turned to face her she was already sitting on top of the island counter, naked, with her legs crossed and the apron hanging from her finger. His dick stiffened immediately at the sight of her.

"Wow," he said, grabbing the crotch of his boxer briefs to adjust his bulge.

Lucky looked down at his boxers and licked her lips before looking him in the eye and biting her bottom lip. She uncrossed her legs to reveal her cleanly shaven pussy, giving him a full view of the treat that he was about to receive. Without speaking another word Reed walked over to her and got in position in front of her pussy. Sticking out his tongue he gently teased her clit, flicking it up and down and then winding it in slow circles. She used her left hand to lean back and her right hand to palm the back of his head. Every so often he'd let out an "Ummmm," savoring the taste of her juices.

Her body was experiencing chills all over as he reached spots with his tongue that no one before him had ever been able to reach. He grabbed both of her ass cheeks to pull her body closer to the edge and allowing him to stick his tongue deeper inside of her moist walls. He was feasting on her pussy like it was his last meal on death row.

"Right there, you're about to make me cum all over you," she whispered. Grabbing his head tighter she moved her hips in a circle and pushed her pussy harder into his face, feeling the early signs of an arising orgasm. It was as if she were running a race and seeing the finish line at arm's length. Just as her body began to shake he slowed down his pace and placed her clit in between his lips and sucked it as if he was French kissing it. She screamed as pure pleasure ran through her veins. She was shaking so much that her movements mimicked a seizure. He pulled himself away, wiped the excess of juices from his face, and quickly revealed his dick before stroking it. She smiled once she was able to open her eyes and focus on him. His dick was the largest that she'd ever seen it and she couldn't wait to fill every inch of it deep inside of her.

"What you know about this?" he asked, referring to his stiff eleven-inch dick. He continued to stroke its length to maintain the hard appearance. He was well aware of her bedroom skills but a little taunting always went a long way. "Bend that ass over so I can get in it," he directed.

Without hesitation she got down off of the counter and turned her ass to him before bending over and arching her back as much as she could. He walked up behind her and pushed her right leg up so that her knee rested on top of the stool. With his left hand he massaged the head of his dick in between the lips of her pussy to feel the wetness before plunging all eleven inches inside of her. A loud moan escaped her lips as her tight pussy gripped his dick. With both hands he grabbed hold of her breasts and with each thrust he'd squeeze them lightly. With her back still arched she pushed back on him as hard as she could to make sure that the head of his dick connected with her G-spot each time he was all the way inside of her.

"Yeah, that's it, tell me how good it feels," he instructed.

"It's more than good, it's great. The best I've ever had," she moaned, stroking his ego.

The sound of her voice intertwined with the sound of his body slapping up against her ass created a melodious atmosphere. He moved in and out of her with ease, making sure to use just enough force to cause just the right amount of friction. He continued the rhythm until she could feel the throbbing of his dick, alerting her of his pending eruption. Soon he held on tight and released every drop of his cum inside of her, which was followed by a loud moan and intermittent tremble. Slowly separating himself from her warm insides, he laughed unexpectedly.

"What's so funny?" Lucky asked, turning around with a look of confusion on his face.

"Just thinking about how good that shit was and the fact that I actually have Raquel to thank for it." He continued to giggle.

"Raquel?" she asked, placing one hand on her hip.

"Yes, because if she wasn't such a bitch I would've never met you." He smiled.

"Oh." She smiled, allowing her hand to ease off of her hip.

"You got me. I'm not going nowhere, all right?" he said before moving close enough to her to kiss her. "All right?"

"All right." She smiled.

"I gotta run out this morning. Romeo is picking me up so you can use my car if you need to go anywhere."

"Okay," she replied.

She watched him disappear into the hallway and soon heard his footsteps going up the stairs. She shook her head and continued to smile, thinking about how happy he made her. She hadn't smiled this much in a very long time and it truly felt good. She was glad that this time she listened to her heart, and after the great morning she planned to make it official and go gather some more of her things to surprise him when he made it back home.

Chapter Fifteen

Choices

"You really should have allowed them to take you to the hospital. Those men really did a number on you," the female detective spoke, entering the interrogation room where Diamond had impatiently sat for eight hours.

"Is this even legal, keeping me here? I mean how many times do I have to go over the story? While my daughter is out there somewhere you're asking me the same questions over and over again," she yelled. She was more than frustrated.

"Listen, if you would have cooperated from the beginning you would have never been here in the first place. If it were me, I'd be doing everything that I could to get my daughter back."

"Sitting here is not going to get her back. I don't have a fucking clue who those men were and I sure as hell won't figure it out locked in this damn room."

"Okay, so let's go over this again and this time I might think about letting you leave."

"I was woken up out of my sleep and beaten. I've told you this. I was taken downstairs where my husband was tied up and beaten. The men made requests for money and I told them that I didn't have any. They murdered my husband right in front of my face." She paused. "Then they told me that they had my daughter and I would only get her back if I came up with five hundred thousand dollars by the end of the week. I didn't think that it was possible then but the likelihood has been cut down dramatically since you've kept me in here, wasting time when I could be trying to gather up the money. The story isn't going to change because that's what happened. I don't understand why you keep asking me over and over again." She stopped and looked at both of the detectives who were sitting on opposite sides of the table.

"So what happened with your first husband? He was murdered too, correct?" the female detective chimed in after a few seconds of silence.

"What does that have to do with anything?"

"Same thing, an intruder right?"

"I wasn't there so I wouldn't know," she yelled.

"What I'm trying to figure out here is how you have such horrible luck that both of your husbands would meet the same fate. Especially when you claim that you didn't have anything to do with it."

"You can't really think I would have my husband murdered. Really, if that were the case would I let them beat me like this? Do you see my face? I look a fucking wreck!"

"I mean I've seen it before. I've seen people get shot or even shoot themselves to cover up a murder. So it's not that uncommon or impossible," she replied, adjusting her position in her chair and leaning forward on the table.

"It's not impossible for a person like me to end up with two dead husbands either. Do you see where I live? There are envious people all over. I loved my husband with all my heart and every time I close my eyes I see his brain being splattered all across the room. There is no way that I would ever order something like that. I love him too much." She said as a tear slowly rolled down her left cheek. She quickly wiped it from her face.

"Listen, I'm really sorry that this has happened to you. I am trying to do everything I can to find your daughter. I want you to believe that, okay? I know she doesn't belong to me but I am a mother and every missing child is just my priority," she said, placing her hand on top of Diamond's hands, which were folded in front of her.

"Please let me go so I can find my daughter. She's all that I have left," she said sincerely while looking the detective in the eye. She realized that being angry hadn't worked so it was time to show her that she wasn't as hard as she appeared.

"I'm going to let you go, but we can't allow you to go out there looking for your daughter alone. After seeing what they did to your husband I don't doubt that they will kill you and your daughter. These people mean business, you have to know that."

"Yes, I know that. I also know that I can't have the police following me around. They'll never give her back. I need to do what they asked of me and provide them with the money. I don't know how I am going to get it but I will figure it out. I just need you to let me go."

"We are experienced with this kind of thing, Diamond, you just have to give us a chance. We've seen a lot of situations turn back real fast when people didn't allow us to do our job. We can set things up so that they will never even know that we're there. We don't have to follow you but we just need to be in the vicinity in case things go bad. We can conceal a wire on you so that we can hear everything that is being said, and we can give you a word to use to signal us if you run into trouble."

"A wire? Hell no. They will probably pat me down and if they find a wire they will kill me for sure. I can't risk that. I need to do it alone."

"If you want your daughter back you will do it our way, Diamond. I understand what you are going through. I know that you feel the urge to protect your daughter but you don't want to be the reason that she winds up dead, do you?" she asked in a concerned tone. She was hoping that her speech would get through to Diamond. She didn't have any evidence to hold her any longer and she couldn't force her to wear a wire, but she knew that it was for the best.

Diamond sat thinking about what the detective said and she was absolutely right, she didn't want to be the reason that her daughter ended up dead. She hoped that once the truth came out, she wasn't the reason that Black was dead, because she wasn't sure that she could live with that guilt. She sat quiet for a few moments, pondering the question that the detective had just asked. She wanted to make sure whatever she said was right.

"Okay, but you have to give me some space. I can't have you on my back."

"We can do that but, again, we need to place a wire on you when you meet them. We can't charge them if we don't have any evidence."

"I understand, now can I go home please?"

"Yes, my partner here will walk you out and here is my card. It has both my office and cell on it. Call me the moment you hear from them, okay?" she said, passing Diamond her business card.

Diamond took the card and placed it inside of her back pocket. She stood up and shook the detective's hand before following her partner out of the room and down the hall toward the elevators. She nodded as the detective waved at her. She understood that they had a job to do but she had one to do as well. Smelling the fresh air she immediately retrieved her cell phone from her purse and dialed the one person she knew would be there for her through thick and thin: Tommy.

"Diamond, what the fuck happened? That shit is all over the news. Where are you?" he yelled through the receiver.

"I'm just leaving the police station. They took me down for questioning. I really need your help, Tommy. Could you come pick me up please? I'm at the Roundhouse."

"All right. I'll be there in fifteen minutes," he replied.

"Okay, see you when you get here," she said before hanging up. She put on her sunglasses and took a seat on the steps to wait for Tommy to arrive. She watched her surroundings, making sure that there wasn't anyone watching her. Her cell phone began to ring, startling her. Looking at the caller ID, it was her mother, Pam.

"Diamond, baby, are you okay? What's going on?" she yelled immediately.

"Mom, I'm okay. I'm just leaving the police station and I'd rather not talk about it out here, so I promise I will call you as soon as I get in a better area."

"Okay, promise me you'll call. I've been worried sick about you. Your father is losing his mind," she yelled.

"Okay, I promise. I will call you back."

"Okay, I love you baby," she replied before ending the call.

Diamond ended the call and placed the phone back inside her purse. She sat patiently waiting for Tommy to arrive, and as promised he was pulling up in front of the building fifteen minutes after they'd hung up. He immediately got out of the car and walked toward her. She removed her sunglasses to allow him to see the damage to her face. Without saying a word he wrapped his arms around her and hugged her. Tears began to fall from her eyes and soak into his shirt.

He held her tightly and whispered in her ear. "I got you now; everything will be okay."

She wanted to believe him, and from previous attempts on her life, he'd been there to save her. Though he'd never spoken the actual words she knew that he loved her, and, deep down, she loved him too.

"Come on, let's get out of here," he said, releasing her from his grip, and he began to guide her toward his car. After closing her door behind her, he walked around to the driver's side and got in. He looked over at her beautiful face, which was covered with cuts and bruises. Her lip was swollen and her hair, which was normally perfectly styled, was matted in spots where blood from her wounds had seeped out and dried up. She continued to cry as she began to try to explain the events that took place.

"They shot him right in front of me, Tommy. I will never get that vision out of my head. They took my baby girl, Tommy." She turned to him with devastation written all across her face.

"What do they want? Was there anything that stood out to you to maybe see who they were?" he asked while merging on to I-76 West.

"They want five hundred thousand dollars by Friday."

"All right, that's not a big deal. I can handle that. But why did the cops keep you so long? Did they think that you had something to do with it?"

"Because I wouldn't stay at the house for questioning. I was focused on figuring out how to get my hands on the money I needed to get my daughter. But when I got there of course she brings up the shit about Kemp, saying that I must be either guilty or really unlucky to have two of my husbands end up murdered."

"Well, they don't have no proof of that, that's why they let you go. That's just formalities and shit, but I think I should take you home so you can get cleaned up and try to get some sleep. Let me deal with getting the money that you need."

"I can't do that, Tommy. I'm afraid that they will think I don't care, like I'm not trying to do all that I can do to get her back."

"Do you think they are watching you? Did they say that?"

"I don't know. They didn't say that but it's very possible, Tommy. After the shit that I went through with Money, hell, anything's possible. You know it's hard to trust anybody. I've been through this shit before," she said, shaking her head. She still couldn't figure out how she'd ended up in this situation. For the past couple of years she'd made it her priority to walk as straight of a line as possible. She wanted to be there for her daughter and not risk this, but Black had other plans, which could have caused him his life.

"So what do you want to do, Diamond? I really think you should try to lie down. I know your body has to be in pain."

"Not in as much pain as I will be in if they hurt my daughter. I don't need to rest, Tommy, but I will go home just to make some calls and change. But I need you to keep in touch with me throughout the day to update me on what's going on. I will do the same."

"Okay, I'll take that," he replied, knowing how stubborn Diamond truly was.

For the remainder of the ride they didn't speak, both of them thinking about the things that needed to be done. Diamond trusted Tommy with her life, but after pulling up in front of her house she instantly felt a rush of emotions. She knew once inside she'd have to look at the bloodstained walls and floors and the spot where Black's body drained of life. She wasn't looking forward to it but she knew that she couldn't avoid it forever. She took a deep breath, hugged Tommy, and exited the car. Tommy watched her enter the house before pulling out of the parking spot.

Chapter Sixteen

Birds and the Bees

Before giving birth to Dior, Diamond never thought that she could love someone as much as she loved her. There was never a moment that she could imagine living without her. Thinking back to her own childhood she remembered two moments: the day her father walked out and the day that she had an abortion as a teenager. Both would mold her future decisions.

"Diamond! Hurry up and get down here for breakfast," her mother yelled through the house. It was almost 7:00 A.M. and the school bus would be there by seven-thirty. She hated waking up so early and she believed her mother hated waking her up just as much. It was always a fight to get her out of the door on time. Her dad was sitting at the table when she got there and, as usual, he and her mom didn't have much to say to each other. Most days they sat across from each other

without speaking a word. She walked to her father's side of the table and gave him a kiss on the cheek. For the first time since she was around five years old he didn't kiss her on her cheek as well.

"Is everything okay, Daddy?" she asked, still standing on the side of his chair.

He set his newspaper down and looked her in the eye. "Everything is fine sweetie. Daddy's just got a lot on his mind that's all." After his response he picked his paper back up off the table and resumed reading it. She knew that something wasn't right but she didn't want to ruin everyone's morning by probing him for more information. She slowly walked away and slid into her seat opposite his. There was a small bowl of oatmeal and a glass of milk sitting in front of her. The air in the room was weird. She couldn't put a finger on what was different but she could feel it in the pit of her stomach. Her mom was standing over the sink washing dishes as they continued to eat in silence.

The date was October thirteenth and she remembered it because of a fire just a few blocks away. One of her best friends lived in that house and hadn't made it out alive. The date seemed significant to her at the time because of the loss, but by the end of that day she would not only lose her best friend but her father as well.

She had just scraped the last bit of oatmeal from the bowl and finished the glass of milk when the long yellow school bus was pulling up outside. She jumped up out of the chair and grabbed her book bag off of the floor. Just as she was about to head to the door her father grabbed her by the arm and pulled her in to a hug. The hug was much different that any other hugs because he wouldn't let go. He held on to her like it was the last hug that she would ever get. After he let go, she kissed him and walked out of the door. She glanced back before stepping onto the bus and noticed him standing at the door with a blank look on his face.

That blank look was one that would haunt her for years, since it was the last time that she'd see his face for the next ten years. She returned home that day and found out that he'd left and wasn't coming back. She also learned that she was adopted. At first, she didn't know how to handle it. In school she was distant and her grades showed it. And if things couldn't get any worse, they lost their house because her mother couldn't pay the bills. They were forced to move in with her grand mom, in a raggedy row home in North Philly.

She hated living there. She was used to having her own room and her own things. There, she not only had to fight for her things, she damn near had to fight for food. Her cousins were bigger and much stronger than her so when it was time to eat she'd quickly be pushed aside and forced to eat the scraps that were left. Then her aunt Cicely was the meanest bitch she'd ever known. Not a day went by when she wouldn't throw in her face the fact that she wasn't really part of the family. As if knowing it weren't bad enough, she had to hear it every day. She would go to bed each night wondering why her real parents gave her away. From the day she found out, her mother tried her best to convince her of how special she was. She couldn't see it, since her biological father and the father she'd always known not only left her but her real mother had as well.

Next there were the boys. She just couldn't get enough of them. She lost her virginity at the age of twelve and had sex with at least five boys by the time she met Johnny. Unlike the rest of them, Johnny couldn't care less about sex. She, on the other hand, was addicted. She loved the feeling of being wanted. The attention that they gave her some how filled the void that her father had left her with. When one would leave, she'd quickly find another one to replace them. This cycle was one of the most reckless she'd taken part in her whole life.

The first time she and Johnny had sex, it was almost like she was a teacher and he was the student. She, Johnny, and Mica were watching TV in their basement. It was cold outside and not much heat was circulating. They were covered up with fleece blankets all piled up next to each other on the sofa. Mica had fallen asleep halfway into the movie and both she and Johnny were wide awake. Hidden underneath the blanket, her hand was rubbing his knee. Soon it was up to his thigh and next she was caressing his package, which was tightly nestled in his underwear. For once, he didn't stop her and since he hadn't, she took full advantage of the situation. He leaned over and began kissing her while palming her over-developed breasts at the same time. By now, she was unzipping his pants and sliding her hand into the opening. She could tell he was excited as his dick grew three more inches than normal. She prayed that he wouldn't stop her as he'd done the few times they'd make it this far. Mica was still sleeping, snoring loudly with drool slowly sliding down the side of her face. They were kissing and tonguing each other down so heavily that you could hear the smacking even over the TV. She stopped him just long enough to ease down on the floor. She motioned with her finger for him to join her. He obliged and within seconds they picked up where they had left off. Instead of getting completely naked she removed just her shorts. Johnny had his pants and underwear pulled down to his knees. She lay on her back as he crawled on top of her and struggled to find her warm opening. With one hand she grabbed hold of his dick and guided it inside of her. He let out a sigh immediately. She knew that he'd never had sex before so she didn't expect him to go very long. Surprisingly, he got into a rhythm and was still going fifteen minutes later. She guessed some men were just born with it because for it to have been his first time he lasted longer than most of the boys she had been with. About twenty minutes later he was shaking and moaning on top of her. She covered his mouth with her hand to muffle the sounds that were escaping it. After they were done, she hurried into the bathroom to wipe herself off and got back in position at the far end of the sofa. Johnny looked over at her and quietly said, "I love you," before focusing his attention back on the movie. She never wanted to tell Mica about their first time. She figured she'd be mad that they did it while she slept a few feet away.

Eventually, she had to tell her and everyone else when she found out that she was pregnant. Her mother was pissed. She didn't understand how she'd managed to sleep with five boys, numerous times each, and hadn't gotten pregnant. She was practically shaking when she told her that she had missed her period. She sat across from her, quiet, while continuing to smoke her cigarette.

"So you missed your period? I guess that wouldn't mean anything unless you were out there screwing. Is that what you're telling me? You've been out there fucking those little boys?"

Diamond was silent, afraid to look her in the eye. She was afraid of seeing the disappointment. What mother would be proud of her teenage daughter carrying a baby?

"I don't hear anything. I just asked you a question." Her voice was louder than it had been a few seconds ago, which to Diamond showed fury.

"I'm sorry, Mom. I didn't think I could get pregnant."

"Why not? Don't you learn that shit in school? As soon as you get a period you can get pregnant. I'm so disappointed in you, Diamond. I expected so much more from you."

Hell, Diamond expected more from herself. She also expected that she'd always have a father around who loved her but obviously that wasn't the case either. She didn't know what to say or do. She did know that she wasn't ready to take care of a baby.

"I'm not ready to take care of a baby, Mom."

"Who said anything about taking care of a baby? I'm taking you to the clinic first thing Monday morning to get rid of it. I'll be damned if you're going to embarrass me."

Diamond sat there with tears forming in the wells of her eyes. She was scared. She didn't think she would force her to get an abortion. She thought they could probably give it up for adoption. She knew her mother very well and what she said was pretty much what happened. There wasn't anything that she could do to make her think any different. Then she thought about it a little more; it was the right decision for all of them. Johnny definitely didn't want her to have the baby. He felt that it would ruin both of them and he probably was right.

That Monday morning, when her mother dragged her down to the clinic in the frigid weather, all she could think about was getting her life back to normal as quickly as possible. The clinic was packed and most of the girls there were around Diamond's age. She figured she wasn't the only one dumb enough to think she couldn't get knocked up. After filling out all of the paperwork, they sat in the waiting *room for hours. It was almost twelve when they finally called her name and they'd been there since seven-thirty in the morning. They led her down a long hall that had bright white paint like you see on TV. Her mother stayed out in the waiting area with the other mothers and young girls waiting for their turn.*

The nurse took her into a small room that had two changing stalls and a bathroom. She handed her a clear bag that contained a hospital gown, socks, and a cap for her head. She instructed her to take everything off, put on the things in the bag, and fill it with all of her belongings. She could barely get her pants unbuttoned she was so nervous. She didn't know what was about to happen to her. They hadn't explained it to her, only saying that her mother wouldn't sign for her to be put to sleep. Is that a form of punishment? How can she force me to be wide awake when they rip my baby from the womb? *she thought. She almost thought about running out of there and hitchhiking a ride home but she probably wouldn't make it past the door without getting snatched back by her mother's death grip. She was so deep in thought that the nurse startled her when she retuned and reached out for her bag of belongings.*

"Come with me. I'll put your things in a locker. I'm going to take you into the procedure room and prep you. Do you have any questions for me?"

"Is it going to be really painful?" She was scared shitless, still unaware of what was about to take place. She knew that she was going to leave there no longer pregnant but she didn't know what would happen between now and then.

"It will be a little painful but doing it without anesthesia is the best way to do it. You won't feel groggy or possibly have any bad after effects. Don't worry, I'll be in there with you the whole time. You can hold on to me and squeeze my hand if you need to."

She felt a little better after that but a little uneasy nonetheless. The procedure room was freezing cold. There was a table in the center surrounded by a bunch of machines. She assumed that most of them were to monitor her vital signs and things of that nature. Just from TV shows and things she'd in school she saw the resemblance. She lay down on the table and tried to relax as she placed her feet in the stirrups and scooted down to the edge of it.

The doctor entered the room a few minutes later in a blue gown and gloves. "This will be over before you know it. Scoot down a little more for me."

She was so uncomfortable. A grown man who was a complete stranger had his face down in her young pussy. She had never even been to a gynecologist before so this was all new to her. She followed his instruction and slid down so that her butt was at the end of the table.

"Okay, now you'll feel some cold fluid. I'm cleaning the area. Now a little pinch."

She damn near jumped off the table. A little pinch my ass, she thought. Whatever he had just done hurt like hell. "Okay, just a few more pinches." She held in the screams as he continued to stick needles in her. Tears were rolling down the sides of her face and landing on the paper that covered the table beneath her. Next came a loud machine and then she heard what sounded like a vacuum. Her stomach was cramping beyond belief. Not even her worst day of PMS felt that bad. After a few more minutes of cramping, the loud machine stopped and the experience was over. She was so weak she could barely stand when the nurse helped her off of the table and into a wheelchair.

She recovered for about an hour before she was allowed to get dressed and meet her mother outside. Once she saw her, she walked around *to the driver side of the car and got in. The ride home was completely silent. She hadn't even asked how she felt. She figured she didn't care since she'd gotten herself into the situation in the first place. She didn't even have the energy to try to spark up a conversation, because she probably wouldn't have joined in anyway.*

Following the abortion, Johnny was afraid to touch her. But the truth of the matter was she wasn't so anxious to have sex either. She'd be damned if she'd go through that shit again. Things between her and Johnny remained the same and she was extremely happy that they did. She'd have been lost without his love or the love of any man for that matter. Being fatherless screwed her up and pretty much set the tone for the way she'd searched for a replacement.

Chapter Seventeen

Sudden Impact

"You wild as hell, Romeo. Straight fool, nigga, you need to be down The Laff House doing stand-up." Reed laughed at Romeo's joke.

"I'm dead serious though, these wretched hoes are so thirsty, and they'll do anything to get wit' a nigga." He continued, "This is real-life shit, no games."

Reed continued to laugh. Laughing and joking with his small group of friends was just what he needed to clear his mind from the events of the past evening. He was hoping that they would update him on his nemesis, Brook, but he was actually glad that the conversation was starting out on a much lighter note.

"I'm surprised we got you out today since you're all in love and shit. Damn, you ain't even run through a few chicks first."

Reed shook his head. "Well I'm sorry I couldn't meet your standards but I'm good." He paused when his cell phone began to ring. "Speak of the devil, here's my baby right here." He smiled before pressing accept. "Hey I was just thinking about you," he spoke, showing almost every tooth in his mouth.

"Hello, who am I speaking with?" a professional male voice responded.

Reed looked at the cell phone to verify that it was Lucky's number and then put the receiver back to his ear. "Who is this? You called me," Reed replied.

"Sir, this is the Philadelphia Police. We found your telephone number as one of the last numbers dialed on this cell phone. Can we ask how you know Olivia Brandon?"

"Olivia is my girl. What is this about, Officer?"

"And what is your name, sir?" the officer asked.

"Reed, Chancellor Reed. Now what is this about?"

"She was involved in a shooting, sir, and she was taken to Temple University Hospital. We weren't able to reach any of her family members so we began to call names of her call list."

"What do you mean? She was shot?" he screamed. He was now on his feet with fear written all across his face.

"Yes, sir, she was shot while driving. You should go to the hospital as soon as you can. An officer will meet you there to ask you a few questions."

Reed let the phone drop to the floor, immediately causing the battery and cover to pop off and fly in different directions.

"What happened?" Romeo asked, walking over to where Reed was standing frozen.

"I gotta get to Temple. She was shot in my car. I swear if this muthafucker Brook is behind this shit I will murder his whole fucking family," he yelled, and bent down to pick up the pieces of his phone.

Romeo quickly grabbed his keys and followed Reed as he stormed out of the door and began making his way to Romeo's car. Romeo got in the car and quickly started the ignition, trying to get him to the hospital as fast as he could. He didn't even know what to say but he knew that he needed to find out what the hell happened. He hoped that Brook wasn't truly behind it because somehow Reed would most likely blame it on him for not taking care of things faster. He decided to keep quiet until Reed sparked a conversation.

He dropped Reed off in front of the emergency room and took his car around the corner to park.

After going to the ER, he wasn't allowed in to see Lucky, so he stood patiently in the waiting room until Reed returned. Reed nodded into the direction of the door and Romeo followed.

"She's in a fuckin' coma, Romeo. Those mutha-fuckers shot into my car ten times, man. Ten fucking times! I know that nigga Brook is behind this shit! Probably thought it was me driving the car, *fuck!*" he screamed. "This shit is all my fault, man, all my fucking fault." He shook his head.

"Damn, man, I'm sorry. Is she going to be okay?"

"She critical right now, man, so I don't know. I left the nurses my number. Let's get outta here. I need some air," he said before walking out of the waiting room doors.

Romeo quickly followed him toward the street. As long as Romeo had known Reed he could only remember seeing him this distraught after the death of his mother. He'd actually said good-bye to his mother ten years earlier in the very same hospital. Reed's mother, Jane, had a husband who abused her on a daily basis. For most of Reed's life he'd have to sit and hear her, or watch her try to cover up bruises with makeup. Once Reed reached his teenage years he would hit the gym faithfully, vowing to get big and strong enough to take on his father's strength.

When Reed was eighteen he moved out of his mother's house, and that decision would be one he regretted to this day, because his father, in a fit of rage, had murdered his mother and then turned the gun on himself. He could remember, as if it were yesterday, when Reed spoke of how he wished he could bring his father back to life just for the satisfaction of killing him. He hadn't even attended his father's funeral. It almost frightened Romeo to see Reed so upset because of past experiences.

After entering the car, Reed sat quiet for a few seconds before breaking the silence. Looking over to his left at Romeo he spoke in a low tone, "Do you have that .45 on you?"

Romeo turned to look at Reed, knowing exactly what he planned to do. Deep down he tried to quickly figure out what he could say to change his mind. "Yeah, I have it."

"You know where he lives at right?" he asked.

"Yeah, I know the spot but—" He was immediately cut off by Reed.

"I need you to take me there right now. I don't need you to try to talk me out of it either. If you don't want to be involved you can drive me there and sit in the car but I'm going to kill this muthafucker. Not tomorrow, a week from now, but today," he said with a serious tone and facial expression.

Romeo had never been one to back out on a friend, especially not one who had always been there for him. He understood Reed's anger and hurt but he didn't want him to end up back in prison or, even worse, dead. So instead of talking him out of it, he made a suggestion. "I'm not going to try to talk you out of anything, but I'm not sure it would be a good idea for us to go there alone, especially not with one gun. Let's ride by and pick up some backup and a few guns."

Reed looked at Romeo and, as angry as he was, Romeo was being more than logical. "Okay, let's do that," he replied.

Romeo exhaled, feeling a lot better about his response, and began the drive to gather up the things they needed to execute the man who, in such a short time, had caused so much havoc.

"Hey, baby, I'm going to head out with the girls. I need to do some shopping," Raquel said as she walked over to where Brook was sitting in the living room with Tone, one of his best friends.

"You always shopping. Ain't shit new, just text me periodically so I know you're okay. I haven't gotten word back yet about that nigga Reed's condition."

"Okay, I will," she said before walking toward the front door. She blew Brook a kiss before opening and closing the door.

Almost instantly there was a loud boom, followed by shattering glass, and Raquel's body was now lying on the floor inside the foyer with a huge hole in her chest. Both Brook and Tone jumped up and reached into their waistbands to retrieve their guns. Raquel lay on the floor, gasping for air before choking up blood and grabbing at her chest.

Within seconds, Reed entered the house, stepping through the broken glass door, holding a Ruger semi-automatic assault rifle in his hands, shooting directly into the living room where Tone and Brook hid behind the sofa for cover. Romeo followed with two other men, George and K-Mack, accompanied by their own heavy artillery. As if his entire body was covered with bulletproof materials, Reed continued shooting without thinking about being shot. Romeo followed closely behind.

George and K-Mack made their way around to the side of the chair where Tone was cowering and both men pumped bullets into his body, killing him. Feathers from the inside of the sofa were flying in the air as if it were snowing inside of the large living room. Brook would every so often reach over the sofa and shoot blindly into the air until realizing that he'd used his last bullet.

"Come on, muthafucker, just get it over with," Brook yelled from the floor.

Reed walked around the sofa and faced him as Romeo, George, and K-Mack stood behind him with their guns raised.

"You tried to kill me, you bitch-ass nigga. Should have made sure it was me behind the wheel and you wouldn't be standing here facing the barrel of a gun."

"Fuck you, nigga, it's no need to—"

Reed shot Brook in the leg, cutting off his statement.

Brook gritted his teeth and moaned in agony. Reed stood in front of him, unmoved. He thought about Lucky and how she didn't have anything to do with the situation that had led them to this moment. Reed allowed him to suffer for a few more seconds before shooting him in his head, taking off part of his face.

The four men immediately left the house, got into their vehicles, and sped off. Once they crossed the Benjamin Franklin Bridge they drove to an old warehouse, where their vehicles were waiting. The men exited the cars they'd driven to the scene and covered them with gasoline before sticking a cloth into the gas tank and lighting them both on fire. They entered the cars and went their separate ways, with Reed and Romeo together in one car.

"Are you good, man?" Romeo asked, concerned about Reed's mental state.

"Yeah, I'm good. Could you run me to the crib to change and then back to the hospital?"

"No problem," Romeo replied.

Chapter Eighteen

On a Mission

"I have the money," Diamond spoke to the caller on the other end of the receiver.

"Good girl. Meet me at the Hustle Chop Shop down South Philly, you know where it is?" Justice spoke in a direct tone.

"Yes, I know where that is. Will you have my daughter—"

Click.

"Okay, now you have to make sure that you keep cool. If you act out of the normal, they will probably get suspicious and that could turn bad. So just be cool; hand them the bag only when you see your daughter. We will be close enough to get to you if something goes wrong," Detective Jones, the female detective who'd been on the case from the start, said to Diamond.

"I hope that you're right with this. I really do," Diamond replied, afraid that things wouldn't go as planned. "Here we go," she said, grabbing the oversized duffle bag that was filled with marked bills.

Diamond left the hotel room located near the Philadelphia Airport. Going to the parking lot she got into her car and began the drive toward the chop shop as instructed. When she arrived her stomach was steadily doing flips. She was afraid to enter for fear of what was waiting for her, but she knew she didn't have a choice if she wanted her daughter. She entered the building, which was empty.

"Hello," she said aloud. Her voice echoed throughout the building.

"Stop right there," a voice called out from the back.

Diamond stopped in her tracks.

Justice appeared from the back of the building, wearing a bandanna covering his nose and mouth, holding a large gun in his hand. "Slide the bag over," he ordered.

"I'm not sliding anything over without seeing my daughter," she yelled.

He began to laugh. "I see you still haven't learned shit. You aren't running shit over here, bitch. I will murder you and your fucking daughter."

"How will I know if she's alive?"

"Because I told you so, that's how."

"Why should I trust you? You have completely wrecked my life in a matter of days!" she yelled in anger. She knew that it probably was her best bet to follow their commands, but there was something in her that wouldn't allow her to go down without a fight.

"Listen, you have two options: live or die. It's totally up to you."

Diamond took a deep breath before speaking, "Well, then I guess you'll have to shoot me in the back because I'm going to walk out of here." She was scared shitless but kept a straight face. She slowly began to turn around.

"Bring the fucking baby out," he yelled toward the rear of the building. Another male all in black revealed himself, carrying her daughter in his arms, and she immediately cried when she spotted Diamond.

Diamond turned around and began to cry. She'd missed her so much and at this point she wanted to hurry up and give him the money and leave with her. Wiping the tears from her cheeks she spoke, "Okay, I have all of the money."

"Slide it over," he ordered again.

Diamond dropped the duffle bag on the floor and kicked it across the floor. Justice bent down to unzip the bag. He looked up at the man holding

Dior and nodded. The masked man passed Dior to Justice and picked up the bag from the floor before disappearing into the rear of the building. Diamond began to walk toward Justice.

"Not so fast," he said, raising the gun.

"I did what you asked me to do. I don't understand." She stopped in her tracks.

"I have a message for you."

"A message?" she asked, confused.

"Yeah, a message from Johnny. You remember him, don't you?"

"From Johnny? What the hell does he have to do with this?"

"Everything. He wanted you to feel the pain that he felt when his sister was murdered. His sister, my cousin, my blood." He removed the bandanna that covered his face.

Diamond looked at him and suddenly his face became familiar. She remembered him and now everything that had happened all made sense. His name was Justice, the younger brother of Deidra, Mica and Johnny's cousin. "I'm sorry about that. I never meant for Mica to be hurt," she cried, trying to plead her case, hoping that he'd spare her daughter's life.

"The tears are pointless. You took someone very dear to me and because of that you deserve to suffer. I could kill you but I'd rather you live with the pain of all the shit you caused. I hope it was worth it. Remember that line? The shit you said before you shot my cousin."

"Please don't hurt her, she's all that I have," she cried.

As she stood there she flashed back to the moment she'd met Johnny and Mica. She'd met Mica through her brother Johnny. Johnny and Diamond met after they both were caught stealing from the neighborhood Shop 'N' Bag. There was a room in the back of the store where they were held until their parents arrived.

Diamond sat there quietly, waiting for her mother to arrive, and watched as Johnny cried buckets of tears. He must have been scared of an ass whooping or something because he was definitely a little extra with his reaction.

"Are you okay?"she asked, trying to get him to stop crying, because he was annoying the hell out of her.

"Yeah, I'm fine!" he replied, turning his face in the opposite direction.

"What's got you so upset? I mean, damn, is the beating going to be that bad?" she asked, still not done probing him for information.

"Why do you care? You don't even know me," he replied.

"I know that but I'm tired of hearing you cry like a little girl, so I'm trying to make small talk to get you to shut up!"

"What?" he asked, turning to look at Diamond.

"You heard me! Stop crying like a little girl," she yelled.

He jumped up out of his chair and ran over to where she was sitting. Soon, they were rolling around on the floor, fighting like two cartoon characters. It was comical seeing them trying to hold the other one's hands down. He wasn't really that much stronger than her, but she didn't really feel like fighting. She simply wanted him to shut up.

"Get your hands off of me," she yelled, struggling to get her hands loose. "I knew you were a little girl. Boys don't fight girls!"

"They do when girls don't know how to keep quiet," he yelled, not releasing his grip on her wrists.

"You know you like it, you like a girl who's slick with the tongue," she said, trying to make him lose his concentration.

"What?" He loosened his grip for a second, and that was all that she needed to get the upper hand. She flipped him over and was now sitting on top of him, holding his hands down.

"Now, why don't you just give up? I got you now," she said, looking him in the eyes as he tried to get loose.

Just then the door opened and his father and sister came in with the security guard from the store.

"What is going on here? Get off of him!" his father yelled.

She quickly got up and moved over to the chair that she had been sitting in before their fight started.

"Nothing, Dad, we were just playing," he lied.

"Just playing my ass. You know how much trouble you're in right now?"

"Yes, Dad," he answered after getting up from the floor.

"Let's go. Don't worry, he'll never steal anything from your store again," his dad said to the security guard as they headed out of the room.

She felt sorry for him because she could tell that he was afraid of his father. It was a few weeks before she ran into his sister. She was walking to the corner store to buy a loaf of bread for her grandmother when she saw Mica. She looked at her strangely before coming over to talk to her. She thought for sure that Mica was going to want to fight since she'd walked in on her and her brother, but she was surprised by what she had to say.

"*You're the girl who was in that security room with my brother, right?*"

"*Yeah, that's me. Why?*" Diamond asked, *preparing for a throw down.*

"*Girl, what's your name? My brother hasn't stopped talking about you since that day. I think he's in love,*" she said, laughing.

Diamond stood there for a second in shock. In love? After the way I talked to him, he must be crazy, *she thought. Then she replied,* "*My name is Diamond. What did he say about me?*"

"*He just said that he liked your style, and you were sly with your mouth but he could deal with that.*"

"*That's crazy, he really said that?*" she asked. Now she was blushing because, though she thought he was a little punk, she thought he was cute. He wouldn't be able to protect me, but he's good to look at as long as he isn't crying, *she thought.*

"*Yeah, he did. My name is Mica and his name is Johnny. We live right over there on Dover Street. Why don't you come hang out with us sometime? We're always outside.*"

"*I might just do that. Thanks, Mica. I'll be seeing you around soon,*" Diamond said before turning to head into the store.

Soon Mica and Diamond were best friends and Johnny was her first love. She found out that their father was extremely abusive and Johnny got it the worst. He was afraid of his father and that was why he cried that day in the supermarket. Johnny was really calm, not like all of the other boys she'd dealt with. Most of them had already had a sample of sex so they didn't really care about quality time and conversation. Johnny, on the other hand, did. They would talk on the phone for hours every night about anything you could think of. During that time Mica and Diamond hung out a lot too. They became really close but grew closer before Johnny got locked up for murder. After years of abuse he was finally fed up and in a rage he shot and killed their father.

Diamond sat on the steps, both eyes full of tears. They had just handcuffed Johnny and taken him off to jail. She was losing her best friend and there wasn't anything that she could do to stop it. Did I cause this? *she thought. If she hadn't pushed him so hard maybe this wouldn't have happened.*

She could remember the blood all over him, when he ran to her house to tell her what happened. It was a vision that she'd never be able to erase.

She heard banging on the back door. It was almost twelve o'clock in the morning so she knew it could only be him. By the sound of the knocks she could tell that something was wrong so she hurried to the door to answer it. It was pouring outside and he stood there in jeans and a T-shirt, soaked with rain and blood. He stood there frozen as she stood on the other side of the threshold with the same look.

"What the hell happened, Johnny?" she asked as tears instantly formed in the wells of her eyes. She grabbed hold of him to make sure that he wasn't hurt.

"I did it. I couldn't take it anymore. I did it," he said as he walked through the door and began pacing. Water was dripping all over the place, leaving little blood-tinged puddles all over the kitchen floor. He was disoriented and filled with anger. She had never seen him so upset. Each time she tried to touch him he'd snatch away and keep repeating the same thing over and over again. She didn't know what it was that he'd done at that moment but she knew it couldn't be good.

"Babe, what did you do?" She was crying at this point. She wanted to console him but at the young age of sixteen she didn't know how. She thought about movies and TV shows to see if she could remember how they'd done it. Her mind was drawing a blank and her instinct wasn't helping much either.

"I did it, I fuckin' killed him. I did it."

"Who did you kill?"

"My father. He can't hurt us anymore."

She couldn't believe what she was hearing. Did he just say he killed his father? *The only thing she could think of doing was holding him. She wrapped her arms around him and held on tight as they cried together. She felt like her world was crashing down. He was going to be taken away and she'd probably never see him again.*

"It's all my fault, I'm so sorry."

"It's not your fault. I had to. I couldn't let him keep abusing us. I had to stand up and be a man."

"Stand up and be a man" was what she'd always told him. She told him that he'd never be a man if he couldn't stand up for himself and protect his sister. She pushed him and now his life was over. She stood there holding him close without saying a word until she heard police sirens and saw flashing lights. A few seconds later there was banging at the door. She opened the door after Johnny gave her a nod. The cops pushed her aside and burst into *the house, immediately putting handcuffs on him. Her mother and aunt had since woken up and were standing in the living room with her. Her mom was clueless as they dragged him out of the house. She cried and tried to free herself from her mother's grip to get one last hug. He was out of the house and into the car before she could get to him. She sat on the steps looking on as they drove away. Her head was buried in her knees.*

"Come on in, baby, and get out of those pajamas. You're soaked."

She didn't budge as if she were glued to the steps. Her body felt like she was drained of the energy that she had.

"Diamond, come on, sweetie. It's late and you have school tomorrow."

School? Is she serious? *She'd just witnessed something that would probably stay with her forever. The look in his eyes when he spoke those words reminded her of those serial killers in movies. There was no feeling behind it. It was as if he didn't care that the man he'd just killed was his father.* How could you murder someone and not give a damn? *She knew that he did it to save them from abuse, but even so he should have cared.*

After a while her mother just sat down beside her and placed her hand on her back. She sat there until she was all cried out and exhausted so much so that she had to lie down.

She didn't get up for school the following morning or the rest of that week. She cried all day and night. She wanted to close her eyes and wake up and it would all be gone. She wanted to be able to hold him at night when he'd sneak over and make love to her. She wanted to laugh with him and smile when he told her how much he loved her. She missed her best friend and letters would never fill the void.

Now all of these years later, she stood face to face with it all again.

"It wasn't my fault," she continue to cry.

Justice displayed a devilish smirk on his face before pointing his gun at Dior's and shooting her.

Dior instantly went limp in his arms.

Diamond began to run toward him, screaming, hoping that what she saw wasn't reality.

Before Diamond could reach him he let Dior's body slip from his hands.

Diamond reached her just as the SWAT team burst into the building and pumped bullets into Justice, causing his body to jerk before hitting the ground.

"Oh God, not my baby, please don't take my baby," she cried, cradling Dior in her arms.

The medics who were on site within two minutes quickly took Dior away in the ambulance while fighting to save her life. Diamond was as quiet as a mouse as the detectives drove her to the hospital. Upon arriving in the family waiting room she was told that Dior was pronounced dead on arrival. She immediately fell to the floor and blacked out.

When she woke up she was staring in the face of Detective Jones.

"I'm so sorry, Diamond, I truly am. If there is anything that—"

"It's all your fault. I could have saved her had you let me do things my way," Diamond yelled.

"Diamond, no one could have predicted what would happen and we did everything by the book."

"By the book? Is that what you call it? In three days I've lost my husband and my child. How can you call anything that happened 'by the book'? I refuse to do this with you right now."

"I will let you rest, however, we still need to talk. I understand what you're going through, Diamond. I will speak with you tomorrow," she replied before turning to leave through the curtain.

Diamond turned her back and closed her eyes, trying to remember the life that she'd just lost. Sadly all she could see was pain and misery.

Chapter Nineteen

Light of Mine

Diamond sat peering out of her bedroom window, remembering how she'd brought Dior into the world. What started out as a plan to hold on to Black ended up making her the happiest woman on earth. Feeling like she was losing Black, she decided that having his child would be the key to keeping him around. She remembered how nervous she was when she read the positive pregnancy test and how she prayed that he would be happy. But just like most things that happened in Diamond's life, nothing went as planned and her plan had almost backfired.

Diamond dialed Black's number before she pulled out of the parking spot.

"What's up?" he said into the phone. He sounded like he wasn't in such a good mood, which might have been even better. She felt like she should be able to brighten up his day with this news.

"You don't sound too happy to hear from me, what's up?"

"I just got a lot of shit on my mind that's all. What's up?"

"Well I have some good news," she said with a huge smile on her face.

"What's that?" he said blandly.

This wasn't going to be as easy as I thought. Whatever is on his mind is really bothering him. *"We're having a baby," she said, excited. He didn't respond. That definitely wasn't the reaction she was hoping for. "Did you hear me? I said we're having a baby."*

"I'm going to call you back in a little while. I have to handle something."

Click.

What the hell? Did he just hang up on me or is my mind playing tricks on me? He didn't just do that. *She stared at the phone, hoping that it would ring again. She felt like bursting into tears. She felt like a damn fool. She couldn't even think straight. She had even begun hyperventilating at one point. She'd gotten so worked up that she had to pull over. She was at the point of no return. What could she do if he didn't want the baby or, even worse, if he didn't want her? That wasn't an option. She questioned if she was overreacting and something really important caused him to end the call so abruptly. She sat there in the car for the next ten minutes before she calmed down enough to maneuver through traffic safely. She made it home and was still out of sorts when she got there. She slammed the door and stomped her feet up to the room like a twelve-year-old. Now she was angry because he hadn't called her back. It was now almost forty-five minutes since he hung up on her. She wouldn't give in and call him again. She wasn't a weak chick. She wasn't even an emotional chick so she didn't know where the hell all of it was coming from. She got up to the bedroom and lay across the bed. She was exhausted and she hoped that maybe if she took a nap, by the time she got up he'd be there apologizing for dissing her the way that he did.*

On the opposite side of town, Black sat staring at the phone and feeling like the biggest asshole on the planet. Did she just say we were having a baby? How the hell did that happen? *He wasn't ready for that. It wasn't that he didn't love kids but with so much shit going on he didn't feel that it was the time to bring a baby into the world. He still had to look over his shoulder every time he took a step to make sure someone wasn't sneaking up on him. He knew she'd be pissed but even more hurt by the way that he reacted, but at the time he couldn't think of anything else to say. He figured not saying anything at all was better then saying the wrong thing. If she was pregnant and planned on keeping it, there wasn't anything that he could say to change her mind. With Diamond that was virtually impossible. Now, he not only had to worry about keeping her safe but a baby as well. And what would Trice do? That was a whole different issue in itself. He could see her becoming more conniving once she got a whiff of the news.*

JB sat across from him, trying to figure out what the hell was going on. His lips were moving but he could no longer hear him. "Hello, is anybody in there?" JB said, waving his hands in front of his face trying to break his stare.

"Yeah, I'm here," he said, shaking out of it for a second.

"Yo, what happened? Who was that on the phone?"

"That was Diamond. I just did some dumb shit."

"What? I was sitting right here and I didn't hear you say anything but you'll call her back."

"Yeah, that's the problem. I didn't say anything. She just told me that she was pregnant and I hung up on her."

He sat back in his chair with a puzzled look on his face. "Damn, that's heavy."

"Tell me about it. I didn't mean to diss her like that, she just caught me off guard. Now I feel like shit because it came across like I don't want it and it's not even like that."

"Well, call her back and explain it. That should settle it right?"

"Man, that shit ain't going to just go away like that. You don't know her like I do and she's not that easy to smooth over when shit gets rough."

"I don't know what else to tell you. Can't say 'buy her some shit' 'cause she can buy anything her damn self."

"Let me show you something," he said as he opened up the drawer and removed the black velvet ring box that he'd locked up inside. He set it on the desk in front of him without opening it.

"Is that what I think it is?" he asked with a surprised look on his face.

"Yeah, it is. Open it."

He sat up and grabbed the box off the desk and opened it. "Damn, man, this shit is tight. Why didn't you give it to her?"

"Because it didn't make sense. We still haven't straightened out this shit with Kemp that's lingering on, and realistically she couldn't marry me if she's still married to him."

"*So you really believe he's still alive?*"

"*I don't know what to believe anymore. I know someone is out there trying to kill me.*"

"*I mean, we were both at the funeral. I know damn well I saw them put his body in the ground. Unless he has a twin, he's dead. I think someone is trying to fuck with you, and by the looks of it they're succeeding. You can't let this shit put your life on hold. If you love her, marry her. She's having your seed now, too, you have to keep it moving.*"

What he said made total sense. Here he was tripping about a nigga he knew for a fact was dead. The whole situation had gotten out of hand and the more he let it get to him the worse things got between him and Diamond. JB was right, that's exactly what they wanted to do. Fuck it, he was going to give her the ring and he was going to do it tonight. I'm not waiting around any longer.

"*You're absolutely right,*" he said, laughing. "*Why am I tripping? I know what needs to be done.*"

"*What about the baby?*"

"*I'm actually excited about that, believe it or not.*"

"*Well, congrats then, nigga,*" he said, standing up to give him dap.

Black grabbed the box back off the table and instead of tucking it back inside the drawer he put it in his pocket. He'd been holding on to it until the right time. And what better time than the present? *he thought.*

Once he left the room he dialed Diamond; surprisingly she didn't pick up. He thought for sure she'd at least answer if only to curse him out. He didn't bother to leave a message; he just headed home to straighten things out. He got up to the door and opened it. It was pretty quiet, but he knew she was home because her car was in the driveway.

"Diamond," he yelled out through the house. He didn't get an answer so he thought she might have been asleep. He walked into the bedroom and saw her stretched out across the bed. She looked peaceful but as he walked closer he could see the dry tear tracks on both sides of her face. Seeing the evidence of her crying made him feel even worse than he had before he got there. He stood there, holding on to his pocket, wondering if it was the right time to pop the question. He wasn't sure if he was ready, and now that he was standing there he was more nervous than he would have imagined he'd be at this point in his life. He stood there for a few more minutes, almost afraid to wake her. She must have felt

his presence because she woke up and noticed him before he was able to leave the room.

"Hey, babe, I didn't mean to wake you." He turned to face her. She didn't respond, only getting up from the bed and heading into the bathroom.

"Diamond, can we talk?"

She stopped in her tracks and turned to walk back to the door. "Talk about what? How you just dissed me? I told you I was having your baby and you hung the phone up." She yelled as she paced back and forth. She had every right to be upset.

"I'm sorry, okay? It just caught me off guard and I wasn't dissing you, I would never do that to you."

"Maybe you didn't want to but that's exactly what you did. That shit was low for you. I never thought you wouldn't be able to take care of your responsibility."

"I can take care of my responsibility. It's not about that. It's really about nothing, I said I was sorry."

She stood there, staring, as if there was something that she wanted to say but couldn't. She shook her head and turned to continue her trip into the bathroom.

"Diamond," he called out to her.

"What?" she yelled with her back still facing him.

"Could you turn around please? I need to show you something." He pulled the ring box from his pocket and opened it.

She turned and looked at him. Still angry and not immediately noticing the ring she spoke, "What is it, Black? I'm really not in the mood for—" She was now staring at the box in his hand. Her frown quickly turned into a smile and tears soon followed that smile. "Are you serious?"

"Dead serious," he said as he walked over to where she was standing. Diamond was never the mushy type and now that she knew she was pregnant that said it all. The crying and the arguments, it was all out of character for her. Some of it he could get used to. Assuming how she felt was based on what he'd done in the past, knowing for sure felt a lot better. He figured this pregnancy had its pros and cons after all. He removed the ring from the small velvet box and placed it on her finger as she held out her hand for him.

Tears were still flowing as she moved in and kissed him. "I'm sorry I'm so emotional. This isn't me. I love you so much. I'm happier than you know." She hugged him.

He felt good, and he hoped that the feeling would last. In the past, he'd been known for losing interest in women after a while but he didn't see that happening with her. Regardless of the ups and downs she was actually one of the only women he felt this strong of a connection to. After a few seconds the smile that brightened her face became dim.

"What's wrong?"

"I'm just thinking about Kemp. We can't get married if he's still alive."

"Look, I honestly don't believe that it's Kemp. Someone else has to know what happened and just wants to fuck with us. I think I know him more than anyone and if he really wanted us dead, trust me, we would have been dead by now. That's real talk, D. I don't see it, I just don't." He shook his head.

"How would someone know what happened? I would have been in jail by now if that was the case."

"Obviously they want something from us, I just have to find out what the hell it is."

"I'm just scared. With the baby coming and all, I don't want anything to happen."

"It won't, trust me. You've believed in me this long, don't stop now. I'm not going to let anything happen to you. I promise." He reached *out to hug her and she obliged, wrapping her arms tightly around him.*

From that point forward Dior was the most important thing in both of their lives. Both of them would give their last breath for her. Diamond couldn't imagine how her life would have been had she never had the joy of being a mother. She would have never thought that she'd only have such a short time to shower her with all of the love that she had for her.

Chapter Twenty

Lost

"Oh my God, Diamond, I'm so sorry. Why didn't you call me sooner?" Kiki said, coming through Diamond's front door. The two embraced before Diamond closed the door. "I can't believe it," she said, shaking her head.

"I can't even close my eyes without seeing it. I have to bury both my husband and my daughter." She fought to hold back tears. She'd been crying so much that she felt dehydrated.

"Well, I'm here for you, girl. Anything that you need me to do I will have your back. Did you make the arrangements yet?"

"No. I actually have to go this evening. My mom and dad are meeting me down there."

"I know how you feel, girl," she said, sitting down on the sofa.

Diamond sat there, looking at Kiki, wondering how she could know how she felt. She'd never lost any of her loved ones, let alone a husband and child. She also wondered why it had taken her so long to come over and show her condolences. It almost made her think back to all of the time that they spent not speaking. She wondered how she could truly call herself a friend and not be there in her times of need. As Kiki sat and talked about how she felt sorry for Diamond and how she could feel her pain, she began to see her lips moving but could no longer hear the words that were coming out of her mouth. She wasn't in the fighting mood, so she decided to sit tight to see what would come out of her mouth.

"I'm just trying to figure out my life and where I'm going. I feel like I'm in a never-ending nightmare," Diamond said with her hands on both sides of her face. She shook her head as quick flashes of the murders crossed her mind.

"Are you okay?" Kiki asked, noticing the sudden change in Diamond's facial expression.

"No, I'm really not okay, but I don't want to keep reliving everything so let's just stop talking about it. What's been up with you? Anything new in Kiki's world?" Diamond asked, changing the subject.

Kiki's face clearly said that something was wrong, but Diamond could never know how what she was about to hear would eventually cause more devastation in life. "He's not around anymore and it's breaking my heart," she replied with a pout.

"What happened?" Diamond asked, concerned.

"Girl, I don't even want to talk about it. It makes me sad. The crazy thing is I've been feeling so sick lately and I think that I might be pregnant, but the way things have played out I'm almost afraid to take a pregnancy test."

Diamond sat, trying to fight back tears. She'd just lost her only child and here Kiki could be carrying a baby. Deep down she felt nothing but jealousy and envy, and at that moment she wanted to run out of the room and tuck her head under a pillow. "Really? Pregnant? I never thought I'd see the day," she said, forcing a laugh.

"Me either. I never thought I'd fall in love either but, hey, life has a way of surprising you."

"You can say that again." She forced a smile. At this point she wanted to get the conversation over with and politely escort her out of the house, but she held it together. Her stomach felt nauseated and her body was numb as she hoped this was all a part of a dream, or better yet a sick joke.

"I don't know. I will probably take a test eventually, but right now I just can't bring myself to do it." She shook her head.

"Well, if you are, you will find out soon enough."

"Yeah. Well, girl, I just wanted to check on you. I have to get down to the club, but if you need me for anything make sure that you call me," Kiki said before getting up out of her seat to go hug Diamond.

Diamond reluctantly hugged her. There was something about Kiki that had changed, something that she just couldn't put her finger on. The warm feeling that she once got from her had turned completely cold. She thought back to the day that she got out of prison and how Kiki was so caring and was right there to help Diamond out of the sticky situation that she'd gotten herself in. The year was 2006 and Diamond had just been released on a drug charge that would change the track that her life would take.

Kiki sat on the sofa, flipping through the channels, when there was a loud knock at her door. Annoyed she quickly got up off of the chair and headed toward her apartment door. "I'm coming, give me a minute," she yelled. She smiled as soon as she opened the door and found her best friend standing there in gray sweat pants and a white T-shirt, and her hair pulled back into a ponytail. "Diamond," she yelled. "Oh my God, I am so happy to see you, girl. When did you get out?" she continued yelling while pulling Diamond close for a hug.

"I just got out today, girl, can't you tell? I look like I just got hit by a bus!" Diamond smiled while walking into the living room of Kiki's two-bedroom apartment.

"Girl, you look better than I thought you would after spending nine months in jail," Kiki said.

"Girl, I'm just so glad to be home. You just don't know!"

"We've got so much to catch up on, like have you even heard from Davey?" Kiki asked about Diamond's ex-boyfriend.

"Hell no, nor do I want to. I know I've said that once before but—" Diamond was cut off by Kiki.

"Once? Girl, you said that when he cheated on you and gave you that STD, when he choked you, hell when he had you in that threesome with his freak-ass baby mom and then had that shit being sold in the streets, and then—"

Diamond cut Kiki off. "Uh I don't need you to remind me, Kiki. I was there, remember? I'm just saying I'm dead serious this time. There is no way in hell I'd go back to him. Those nine months I did in jail for him gave me a lot of time to think," Diamond said, shaking her head.

"Well um, I hope you thought about seeing Gia at the salon because your hair is tore up, *and now that I'm looking at it close, it looks like a bird made a nest in it."* Kiki laughed.

"Shut up, I'm going, girl, as soon as I get me some money. And, speaking of money, I heard about this dude named Kemp when I was locked up. Do you know him?" she asked with a huge smile on her face.

"Kemp, yeah. Who doesn't know him? He's only the richest hustla in the city."

"Well, I mean what's up with him? Does he have a girlfriend?"

"Yeah, last I heard he did, but that's not the guy you want to get involved with. You just got out of a bad relationship," Kiki said, concerned.

"I'm not looking for love this time, Kiki. I'm trying to get paid."

"Just be careful, whatever you do. I've heard some bad things about him."

"I'll be fine, trust me. You know I can take care of myself."

"Like you did with Davey?"

"You don't have to try to play me, Kiki. I know I've made a lot of dumb mistakes in my life but I thought you were my friend."

"Listen, I am your friend, probably the only real friend that you have. Look, a friend is one who knows who you are, understands where you have been, and accepts what you have become.

Chapter Twenty-one

Chance Meeting

Diamond sat at the bar, sipping an apple martini alone. Lately, she'd been trying to find a way to clear her mind without having to hear other people's opinions, thoughts, or concerns about her or the events that had taken place. She'd buried her family and now she stood alone, trying to figure out what it was she wanted to do with her life. She looked at her watch, noticing that she had just a few more hours before she met with Tommy to square all of their business stuff away. Knowing that she should probably have a clear mental status, she couldn't bring herself to deal with anything sober. Somehow, the alcohol would help block out some of the bad things that clouded her brain.

"Is this seat taken?" a deep male voice said in her ear.

"No," she said without turning around to face him.

"I'm sorry to be forward, but I'm wondering why a beautiful woman like you is sitting here all alone? And looking so sad."

"I just like spending time alone without anyone talking to me."

"Oh, I'm sorry. I don't mean to bother you. I just wanted to see if there was anything that I could do to brighten up your mood, that's all."

"I doubt very seriously if you could help me but thanks anyway."

"Well, Diamond . . . That is your name, right?"

"How did you know my name?" she asked, immediately paranoid.

"The earrings." He laughed. "I'm not a stalker or anything."

Diamond laughed, feeling silly.

"Look, my name is Chance. If you would let me buy you a drink, I will leave you to your drinks if you'd like me to. I just wouldn't feel right walking away without at least trying to give you something to smile about."

"Well, I guess one drink won't kill me," she replied, finally taking a look at the handsome stranger.

"Cool. Bartender, can you bring her another round please?" he yelled to the bartender.

"Thank you," she said.

"So, Ms. Diamond. Are you in a relationship? Married?" he asked.

"I was married but I lost my husband."

"Sorry to hear that, I really am. I wish that I could take that pain away because I can see in your eyes that it's still hurting you." Chance smiled.

"I'd rather not talk too much about it but I can appreciate your concern."

"I understand. I won't push the issue. Let's change the subject. I really think that you are a beautiful woman and I would like to take you out to dinner sometime if that's okay with you."

"Uh I'm not sure if—"

"I'm not asking you to marry me. I'm asking for one harmless dinner."

"Umm, I don't know." She shook her head.

"Please just one dinner. If I'm the biggest asshole on the planet then by all means, walk away."

Diamond sat silent for a second, pondering the question that he posed. He was trying to convince her that he was her Prince Charming but she wasn't biting as fast as he thought that she would. Diamond looked down at her watch, knowing that Tommy would be there any minute to scoop her up for their meeting. She didn't want him to walk in and catch her talking to another man so soon after Black's death. Not that she owed anyone an explanation, but she still wasn't in the mood for anyone's opinion.

"Okay, one date; that's all that I will promise," she blurted, trying to hurry up and get rid of her uninvited guest.

"Cool. Well, here's my card. I will let you go so you can get on with your day. I really hope that I didn't bother you too much or take up too much of your time," he said before grabbing her hand and kissing it on the back of it.

She allowed him to kiss her hand before quickly pulling it away.

"Give me a call, Ms. Diamond, so we can set something up." He began to walk away.

"Will do," she replied. She didn't have any intention of calling but she entertained it long enough to get him to walk away. He was cute though, there was just so many things going on that she found it hard think about being with a man. It wasn't that he wasn't attractive or that she didn't see his politeness as something that she could get used to, she just wasn't ready for a relationship as she was still trying to cope with her losses. She turned around to finish her drink when Tommy walked into the bar and headed in her direction. He immediately hugged her once he got near her.

"We need to go somewhere else and talk," he said with seriousness written across his face.

"Why? What's wrong? I don't like the way this sounds," she replied, immediately nervous.

"Come on. I will tell you in the car," he said, gently grabbing her by the arm. He pulled out a one hundred dollar bill from his pocket and threw in on the bar to cover Diamond's bill.

She could barely wait to get in the car before questioning him again. He entered the car and his ass was barely planted in the seat before she began to speak. "What is it, Tommy? What's going on?" she asked.

"I don't know how to tell you this." He paused.

"Just tell me, Tommy, whatever you have to tell me."

"I promised Black that I would be here to take care of you in the event that anything ever went wrong and he wasn't here." He sat quietly, thinking back to his promise to Black.

"So how does it feel?" Tommy asked, raising his glass to Black's.

"It feels good, man, it feels damn good." Black laughed. They were out celebrating because business was back on track. Money was flowing in and the soldiers were all in line. He never thought he'd be enjoying this moment with Tommy. Thinking back, all he could think of

was Kemp and how he promised him that he was destined for greatness. He used to feel bad about being with Diamond but now he didn't. He knew that this was the way that things were supposed to be.

Black looked over at Tommy and smiled before speaking. "I remember sitting with Kemp when he made a million dollars. We were sitting in his living room and we had a bottle of champagne sitting on the table. We were both pretty drunk and Kemp said to me, 'A million muthafucking dollars, do you believe this shit, nigga?'"

"I knew you'd do it, you always said that you would."

"He said, 'I sure did and you're getting to enjoy it with me. Being on top is a wonderful thing and you'll be here one day.'"

"I feel you and I'm happy to witness this shit for real. I was speaking from the heart because honestly I was just as happy for him as I would've been had the roles been reversed"

"I'm king of the world, nigga, ain't that what they say! Kemp was standing on top of the sofa with a glass in his hand all drunk and shit like Nino in New Jack City."

"That's what they say." I was cracking up at him by this point. This nigga was drunk as hell and spilling shit all over himself and me." Black said.

"On some real shit though"—Black sat back down next to Tommy—*"when I'm dead and gone, you're the only nigga I'd want to have this shit. Even down to my bitch, you can have it all. I mean that shit, man; I love you like a brother."*

"I love you like a brother too."

"Let's drink to that shit then," he yelled as he grabbed the bottle off the table. *Instead of pouring it, he toasted his glass with it and drank the rest of it. Black laughed that night but he believed that what he said was true. If there was anyone he wanted to have all that he accomplished when he was gone, that person was Black. He felt good knowing that he wouldn't have wanted it any other way.*

Now, he had it all. Everything that was his, even his woman, was now Black's. Tommy looked at him and began waving his hands in front of his face to break his stare.

"Yo, what the hell are you thinking about, man?" He laughed as he turned to look at him.

"I was just thinking about Kemp and something that he once said to me. He told me that I would have everything that was his when he was dead and gone."

"What the hell made you think about that?"

"Because I used to feel bad about being here and I felt like I didn't deserve it."

"Man, if anybody deserves it you do. You deserve it all, even Diamond."

Black looked at him and just nodded his head. At least there was someone on this earth who felt the way that he did. He looked back on his life and the way that things had turned out. He was satisfied with that and he was looking his future in the eye, ready to take it head on. Now looking at Tommy and knowing what he'd done for him he could see how Kemp felt the way that he did back then. Black lifted his glass and turned it in Tommy's direction.

"In the words of Kemp, when I'm dead and gone there's no one else I'd want to have everything that's mine. Even my woman or bitch as he'd say." Black laughed. "On some real shit, Tommy, that person is you. When I'm not here it's all yours and I mean that shit from the heart."

Tommy looked at him as if there was something that he wanted to say. He wasn't sure what the look was for but he sat silent for a minute or two before he raised his glass to Black's, looked at him, and said, "That's real shit, and I'll handle it with care!"

"What is it, Tommy. I can't take it anymore," Diamond yelled, breaking his moment of silence.

"I got word that Johnny is behind the murders of Black and Dior. I—" He was cut off by Diamond.

"What? Johnny? I can't believe that, Tommy. Why would he do that, Tommy? He loves me."

"Correction, Diamond, he loved you. That's some little puppy-love shit that went out the window the moment you shot his sister."

"He wasn't a street dude, Tommy. Who does he even know who would do that?" she asked, still trying not to believe that her first love had ruined her life.

"You meet a lot of people on the inside, Diamond. I got this info from a reputable source and they told me that he planned all of this shit with some nigga named Reed who was paroled. I haven't located Reed yet but I have people out trying to find out who the hell he is."

"I can't believe this, Tommy. This shit is all my fault." She began to cry. "What am I going to do? Does this mean that he wants me dead too?"

"I don't know, Diamond, but you don't have to worry about that. I have your back and I'm going to make sure that no one can hurt you." Tommy reached out to hug Diamond in an attempt to console her.

"Am I even safe in my home?" she cried.

"I'm not taking you home. I'm going to take you to my house and I will have someone watching you anytime that I have to leave. I'm taking you there now. I really don't want you to worry about this. If you know one thing about me it's that I keep my word and I promise you I will get everything under control. Do you trust me?" he asked, staring her in the eye.

"Yes, I trust you," she said, wiping the tears from her cheeks.

"Okay, let's go." Tommy turned on the car and pulled out of the parking spot, heading toward his house. He had a lot of things to take care of and planned on keeping her safe by any means necessary.

Chapter Twenty-two

Expect the Unexpected

"Where are you going?" Tommy asked as Diamond emerged from the bedroom wearing a short black dress that hugged all of her curves.

"Uh last time I checked I was grown, Tommy," she replied with a twisted lip.

"Diamond, I can't protect you if you're going to just run around the street unsupervised. Looks like you have a date or something to me with that tight-ass dress on," he replied with a bit of force in his voice.

"As a matter of fact, I do have a date, Tommy, and I really appreciate you keeping watch over me and all, but you're not my father or my man, okay?" she said, heading toward the bedroom door. Since meeting Chance, Diamond had decided to give him a try even if just to keep her mind off the drama for a little while.

"I'm not your man yet," he replied, stopping her in her tracks.

"Yet? What the hell does that mean?" She turned around to face him.

"It means exactly that, Diamond. Come on, you know how I feel about you, and there is no way that I'm going to sit back and watch you ride off into the sunset with the next nigga when I've been down for you since day one."

"I can't do this with you right now, Tommy, I'm already late."

"Well, I will be here when you come back, believe that. This conversation isn't over, and your little date, he may have won you for the night, but I'm sure to win you for the rest of your life."

She stood there with chills running through her body. She'd tried for years to hide her own feelings because of Black, and now that Black was gone there wasn't anything keeping them apart besides her. Tommy made it loud and clear that he wanted her but she fought with herself to give in, and decided to go on with her date, thinking that maybe she'd be able to deal with it better when she returned or, better yet, maybe he'd forget all about it. Instead of responding she turned and walked out of the room.

Tommy didn't bother to follow her, confidant that things would work out in his favor. He grabbed his cell phone from the pocket of his jeans and dialed Tip, one of the men he'd hired to keep an eye on Diamond.

"Yo," Tip yelled into the receiver.

"She's on her way out. I need you to follow her," he instructed.

"Got it," he replied before ending the call.

Diamond exited the house and looked over at Tip's car before she hit the alarm on her own car. She was certain that Tommy had already instructed him to follow her but she didn't plan on letting any of that ruin her evening. She was on her way to meet the mystery man who went by the name of Chance. Since the night that she'd met him almost a week prior they'd kept in contact via phone. She was excited to finally get out and have that companionship that she'd missed since Black's murder. Unaffected by Tip's trailing vehicle she blasted her Beyoncé CD and sang every word.

She arrived at the restaurant twenty minutes later, only five minutes later than she was supposed to. She walked into the dining room to find Chance already seated. He stood from the chair when the hostess escorted Diamond over to the table. He was dressed all in black with Gucci sneakers and a Gucci belt to match. His watch almost blinded her as she approached. He immediately reached out to give her a hug and gently inhaled, smelling the fragrance that she had generously applied before leaving the house.

"You look beautiful," he said, looking her up and down.

"Aww thanks, you look very handsome tonight." She smiled.

After they were both seated he didn't waste any time sparking up a conversation. "I couldn't wait to see you tonight. I couldn't stop thinking about you ever since we met."

"If you're trying to make me blush, it's working. I can appreciate a man who knows how to make me smile." She giggled.

"Oh, I'm a professional at that. Shit, that's listed on my business card." He laughed. "But naw, really, I think that you are one of the sexiest women I've seen in a long time. I'm really glad that you decided to come out with me."

"Well, you were practically stalking me." She laughed.

"Oh, you gonna play me like that, huh?" He laughed.

"I'm just being honest," she joked. "But tell me more about yourself, Mr. Chance, because right now there's a bit of mystery and I'm not sure if I'm one hundred percent comfortable with that."

"Mystery?"

"Yeah," she replied with a smile.

"Well, Ms. Diamond, there isn't much to know about me. I'm a hustler by nature, a fighter by necessity, a gentleman by experience, and a provider by mentality. Does that it explain it all?" He paused.

Diamond sat there without a word. She wondered if dancing around the question was a bad sign. She hadn't been able to get many clear answers out of him since she'd met him. Most of their phone conversations had been about her and most of the time he'd find a way to turn the attention back on her whenever she tried to give him a survey. The more that he avoided her questions the more she'd ask. She wasn't giving up that easily.

"No, that doesn't explain it all; that's all superficial if you ask me. I'm trying to find out about the man inside, the things that you can't see from the outside. All of that is skin deep."

He began to laugh before speaking. "Diamond, you're funny as hell, but real, and I can appreciate that. We'll have plenty of time to talk about me. I'm just merely trying to enjoy this date. I mean you only promised me one date so why not enjoy it?"

Diamond shook her head, realizing that he was obviously more stubborn than she thought. She glanced over to the bar and noticed Tip sitting there with a glass, watching her. She immediately became annoyed but because she didn't want Chance to realize his presence she tried to play it off as if she'd never seen him.

"What's wrong?" he asked, noticing the quick change in her facial expression.

"Oh, nothing, I thought I saw someone I knew that's all."

"Don't worry. I know your guard dog is over there keeping watch. Don't fret, it doesn't bother me. I know all about your husband's murder so I expected some extra company on this date."

Shocked she replied, "Huh? How did you?"

"I know more than you think I know, Ms. Diamond, and soon you'll know more about me. But let's continue this date and make the best of it. If he wants to watch, let's give him a show." He leaned across the table and grabbed Diamond by the chin before softly kissing her on the lips.

She didn't resist, as his lips were as soft as butter and as sweet as honey. Tip stopped drinking his drink and picked up his cell to make a call to Tommy to update him on the scenery.

"Yo," Tommy yelled into the receiver.

"I'm sitting here watching her, and this nigga just kissed her. I think he knows that I'm watching."

"Who is this muthafucker anyway?" Tommy yelled, immediately annoyed.

"I don't know. I'm gonna snap a picture and send it to you. In the meantime I'll keep a close watch and I will hit you back if I see anything else."

"Make sure she doesn't go home with this nigga either. I need to find out who the fuck he is."

"Okay," Tip agreed before hanging up the phone.

Diamond and Chance continued their conversation unaffected by Tip's presence. As promised, he calmly snapped a photo of Chance from his cell phone and sent it to Tommy. Diamond was beginning to enjoy the conversation. The two sat and talked in between bites. Neither of them was really interested in their meals as their exchanges were enticing. The waitress has since dropped of the check as the two continued their conversation.

"So what made you want to talk to me?" Diamond asked.

"I thought I already told you. You caught my eye when I first walked in. You were the most beautiful woman in the building and I just had to have you."

"Have me? Is that right?" she said, placing her hand on her hip.

"Yeah, that's what I said. Look, I'm a cocky nigga and I know it. My conversation got you here with me tonight so I know that it will get you to my house eventually."

"Oh, really?" she said with attitude, though she was impressed by his confidence.

"Really. I don't go at anything without the intention of coming out a winner. I plan on taking home the trophy and that trophy is you."

"Trophy, huh? Is that all you see me as? I've been a trophy wife before, not really trying to go that route again."

"Not at all. I'm just saying I'm going to win you over, you'll see."

"And what about tonight? What are your plans for this evening?" she asked with a smile.

"This evening, I've already done what I wanted to. I just wanted to entertain you. I'm not trying to get you in the bed tonight, but that's damn sure my plan eventually."

She laughed, but deep down she was hoping that he would have taken her home. She could definitely use a bit of sexual healing. "I'll accept that," she replied.

"Cool. Well, let me walk you to your car then so your watchdog can sit." He began to laugh.

Chance placed two crisp one hundred dollar bills on the table to take care of the bill and tip.

"Okay," she agreed.

Chance walked her to the car and gave her a long hug before backing away and kissing her once more. She got in the car with a huge smile on her face. For the first time since Black's and Dior's deaths she finally had something to look forward to.

She headed back to Tommy's house, though she wanted to go home. She knew that it would be a night filled with argument if she went anywhere else besides his house, and she wasn't really in the mood for fighting after such a great night.

After pulling up in front of Tommy's house she waved at Tip, who pulled up just behind her. She wanted him to know that she knew he was trailing her. She entered the house and took her shoes off at the door, hoping that Tommy was asleep.

"So you had a nice time?" Tommy said, appearing from the dark living room.

"Damn, Tommy, you scared me. Why are you hiding in the dark and shit?" she asked, walking over to turn on the light.

"I'm not hiding. You see me don't you?"

"Yes, I see you, Tommy. Thanks for almost ruining my date having Tip practically sitting at the damn table."

"I do that because I care about you, Diamond. I don't know why the hell you needed a date anyway when I'm right here," he said, moving close to her.

"Please, Tommy, I'm really tired," she said as she backed away, trying to avoid letting the feelings she had for him rise to the surface.

"Diamond, stop fighting me. I know that you want me just as much as I want you." He moved in closer, backing her up against the wall.

"Tommy, please." She resisted as he grabbed her by the waist and leaned his body on hers, forcing her to stand still.

Without warning his lips touched hers. He moved them from side to side, rubbing them against his, savoring the moment before gently forcing his tongue in between her lips. Once his tongue met hers she obliged, no longer fighting him. She could feel his dick rising in his lounge pants, bumping up against her pussy. She felt her panties getting moist as the kiss began to get more passionate. He used both of his hands to lift her dress above her waist and grabbed both sides of her lace thong and pulled them down. He quickly turned her around to face the wall and dropped his pants in one swift motion. He backed up toward the chair that sat against the wall in the hallway and sat down, pulling her on top of him. Her pussy was soaking wet as his dick slid deep inside of her. He lifted up off of the seat slightly as she moved up and down on his dick.

"Oh shit, Diamond. Damn this pussy is so wet," he said aloud.

Besides a few moans she silently rode his dick like a rollercoaster, trying to avoid screaming as the girth of his dick was much bigger than she was used to. She used the handles of the chair as leverage, afraid to let him fill her completely.

"Don't run from this dick, take it all," he said, trying to lift his body to go deeper inside of her. He moved his body in a circular motion until she let out a load moan, followed by the trembling of both of her legs. "Are you cumming, baby?" he asked.

"Oh shit, oh shit," she moaned, feeling her cum running out of her body and down the shaft of his dick. Her walls were contracting around his dick as he quickly stood her up and bent her over the chair with his dick still buried inside of her. With his hands forcing her back into a deep arch he pumped his dick in and out of her with force causing his body to slap loudly against her ass. He drilled her like a machine, causing her to cum three more times before he exploded inside of her.

"Boy, I don't know what you are trying to do to me," she said as he stood her up and embraced her from behind with his dick still inside of her.

"I'm trying to make you love me, that's all," he replied. "I'm not done yet though. I just want to get you up to the bed so I can really get inside of you."

"Well, come on and finish what you started," she said before forcing him to release his grip. She walked toward the stairs and used her finger to motion for him to follow.

He laughed looked up to the ceiling and said, "Thank you," before following her up to the bedroom. Though the night didn't begin as he planned, it couldn't have ended any more perfectly than it had.

Chapter Twenty-three

The Unimaginable

"I hope she's here," Jasmine said to Octavia as they stood on Diamond's step. They'd been looking for her for the past three weeks, trying to give her the word on the street. They finally saw her car parked in the driveway and took a chance at knocking. A few seconds later Diamond opened the door, dressed in a long maxi dress and a pair of jeweled flats.

"Girl, we've been looking everywhere for you," Jasmine said, giving Diamond a hug. Octavia followed her, making her way into the foyer of Diamond's house.

"What's so important, ladies? You know I've been trying to get shit settled over here. What's up?" she asked.

"Have you heard from Kiki?" Jasmine asked, sitting down on the sofa.

"No, I haven't heard from her. Why?"

"So you haven't heard either?" Jasmine asked with a look of fear in her eyes.

"I think you should sit down," Octavia chimed in.

"Sit down for what? Just tell me. What is it?"

"Well, word on the street is your girl Kiki, your supposed-to-be sister, supposed-to-be best friend in the world—"

"Just spill it, Jaz," Diamond cut her off.

"That baby she's pregnant with, she's been going around telling everybody that Black is the father, and they were having an affair for over two years before he died."

"What?" Diamond raised her voice.

"Yup, she's telling everybody how he was going to leave you and everything," Octavia said.

"Where did you hear this? That can't be true. Black would never do that to me, he loved me too much," Diamond said as she sat down in the chair and placed her hand on her chest in disbelief. Now she had to face the truth. It was one thing to suspect and another to know but now everyone knew and Diamond refused to look like a fool. She couldn't have her image tarnished any further.

"Diamond, I wish that I didn't have to be the one to bring you the bad news but it's true. She's been freely telling everybody, Diamond. I told you that bitch was bad news," Jasmine replied.

Diamond sat silently, trying to take it all in. She didn't know whether to cry, scream, or yell. The pain that shot through her body was unlike any that she'd felt before. How could she move forward if everyone was behind her back laughing at her? How could she look Kiki's baby in the face and not remember her own? Her head was spinning and as Jasmine continued to talk, she could no longer hear her. After a few seconds she interrupted her. "Do you know where she is right now?"

"No, but I can certainly find out," Jasmine replied, retrieving her cell phone from her purse.

"Okay, well I need you both to go with me to see her. If I go alone I may end up in prison tonight."

"No problem," both of the ladies said before they all got up and headed toward the door.

As usual, Tip was sitting outside in his car. He noticed the three ladies walking toward Diamond's car and tuned on his ignition to begin to follow her. The women drove to Kiki's house and parked. Diamond jumped out of the car and walked to the door, banging on it as if she were the police.

"Hold on, damn," Kiki yelled from the opposite side of the door. She walked to the door and opened it without asking who was on the opposite side. As soon as she opened the door Diamond punched her in the nose, causing her to fall to the floor. Diamond quickly got down on top of her and punched her in the face repeatedly.

"You trifling-ass bitch! All of the men in the world and you had to fuck mine. I should kill you, you fucking bitch," she yelled, banging her head into the floor. Blood was pouring from Kiki's nose and lips. Kiki tried to push Diamond off of her but fueled with hurt and anger she overpowered her. Jasmine and Octavia sat and watched, allowing Diamond to take all of her frustration out on Kiki's face.

Outside, Tip heard the commotion and ran over to the house, pulling Diamond off of Kiki. Diamond kicked her as she was being pulled off of her. "Let me go, Tip," she screamed. "If I ever see your fucking face again, bitch, I'll kill you," she screamed. "The only man I ever loved, you just had to have him."

Kiki got up from the floor, silent, trying to recover from the beating that she'd just taken.

"Let me go," Diamond continued to scream.

"Get her out of my house before I have her arrested." Kiki finally spoke, holding her stomach with one hand and the side of her face with the other.

"Diamond, let's go," Tip yelled, pulling her toward the door.

"I'll go for now but this isn't over," she said calmly, pointing in Kiki's direction. She turned to the door as if she was going to walk out, but the second that Tip released his grip she ran past him, Jasmine, and Octavia and punched Kiki in the face again, knocking her back to the floor. "Now we can go," she said, walking out of the door.

Tip shook his head and walked behind her to her car. "You're crazy as hell, Diamond," he said with a laugh.

The three women got in Diamond's car and drove back to Diamond's house, where Chance was sitting on her steps. Jasmine and Octavia looked at each other and then back at Diamond. "Who is that?" Jasmine asked.

"That's Chance, he's a friend of mine," she replied with a smile, as she was happy to see him. She'd been spending a lot of time with him but she always had Tip lurking at Tommy's command, making it hard for them to get close.

"Chance? I heard that name before. Where do you know him from?" Octavia asked.

"I met him at the hotel bar downtown."

"I can't remember where I heard that name but have fun. Hope he can make you smile after the shit that we just told you," Octavia said before exiting the car.

"Well, thanks for telling me. I'm glad I didn't hear it from the streets."

Jasmine and Octavia hugged her before walking to Jasmine's car and leaving. Diamond waved and walked up the driveway to her steps to hug Chance, who stood when she got near him.

"I thought we were meeting at five," he said, kissing her on the forehead.

"I know. I had to go handle something. Sorry I'm late."

"Is everything okay?"

"Now that I see you, everything is just fine."

"Cool. So are we going now?" he asked.

"Yes. I just need to run in the house and grab something really quick. Come in," she said while waving her hand, directing him to the door.

"Are you sure? I'm finally invited into your castle?" he asked, holding both of his hands in the air.

"Yes, you are invited." She laughed before walking to the door and opening it.

He laughed and followed her inside. "Very nice," he said, looking around as if he'd never seen the inside of her home before. He immediately looked into the dining room and flashbacks of Black's body came across his eyes. He knew that he had to deal with Diamond just until he found out where she kept the money. Since their plan hadn't gone as they'd hoped, he ended up coming out of the deal empty-handed. He was furious when he got word that the exchange hadn't gone off as planned. He waited patiently by the phone only to see it all play out on the news. Sure, Johnny got exactly what he wanted. She would always have to suffer with the thought of knowing that she was the reason her family was gone, but he didn't get the money that was promised and he planned to get it by any means necessary.

"What's wrong?" she asked, noticing him staring into the dining room.

"Oh nothing, just admiring the décor." He laughed. "Everything here is just as beautiful as the owner." He smiled.

"You just love to compliment me." She laughed. "I'll be right back. I'm just going to run upstairs really quick."

"Okay, I'll be here."

She ran up the stairs and heard her cell phone ringing as soon as she reached the top of the stairs.

"Hello," she yelled, out of breath.

"Are you fucking him?" Tommy yelled.

"No, Tommy, I'm not fucking him. Why are you so loud?"

"Well, what is he doing in the house, Diamond? That wasn't part of the plan."

"I had to get something, Tommy, calm down," she whispered as she walked into her room and closed the door.

"I don't want you in a closed place with him, you hear me? I need you to get back outside to a public area where Tip can see you."

"Okay, I'm going, Tommy."

"All right, come to my house when you're done."

"Okay," she replied.

"I love you, Diamond," he said before hanging up.

She put the phone into her bra and walked back out of the room to find Chance standing in the hallway.

"Are you okay?" she asked, shocked.

"Just looking for your bathroom."

"Oh, it's right there on the left," she said, pointing to the open door.

"Cool," he said, walking to the bathroom and closing the door.

Her heart was beating a mile a minute. Just a week prior Tommy had told her about his true identity and what he was there to get. She had to continue to act as if she was falling for him to avoid getting hurt. Tommy wanted to be sure that there weren't any other assailants before taking him out. To stare at the man who had a part in her husband's and daughter's murders made her sick to her stomach. She wanted to just murder him herself but she decided to allow Tommy to lead this time. Things hadn't always gone good for her when she tried to handle things on her own. She was nervous that he'd realize she was on to him and lose her own life, but she kept it as cool as she could when he exited the bathroom with a smile on his face.

"Are you ready?" he asked.

"Yup," she replied.

The two left the house without incident and got into his car to head out for dinner. He looked over at Diamond and noticed that she was uneasy. He couldn't figure out what was on her mind but he was determined to find out one way or another.

"Are you sure you're okay? You haven't been acting like yourself."

"I'm fine really. I just had an eventful day that's all."

"Anything you want to talk about? You know I'm here if you need to let off some steam."

Realizing that he wouldn't let up easily she decided to tell him about the Kiki incident to deter him from the real reason she was so jittery.

"Well, I just learned today that my one-time best friend is pregnant with my deceased husband's child."

"Wow, that's heavy. Damn, Diamond, I'm sorry you have to deal with that shit. Did you talk to her?"

"No, I didn't talk to her, but I beat the shit out of her. That's why I was late meeting you."

"Damn, I'm sorry about that, baby girl. That's real fucked up but that's why you can't trust people. They'll always backstab you for their own gain."

She looked over at him and shook her head. Hell, she couldn't trust him either. It was almost as if everyone in her life was out to get her. She didn't know what to believe, or whom she could depend on. The only person who had been there for her from the beginning was Tommy, and she couldn't wait until this was all over with so she could let him know just how much she appreciated him.

"But I'm fine. I don't want that to ruin our evening."

"Well, I'm glad that you're okay," he replied.

After dinner Chance drove Diamond home with every intention of getting back inside of her house. He wasn't concerned about the watchdog or anyone he would bring with him. He needed to make her as comfortable as possible to find out all that he needed to know.

Once they were in front of the house she had to figure out how she would end the night.

"So am I invited in again?" he asked, standing in front of her on the steps.

"Uhhhh, that depends on what you plan to do once you're in there," she said in a sexy tone.

"Well, that's for me to know and you to find out, but, trust me, you will enjoy it." He smiled and moved closer to her.

She looked over at Tip and gave him the signal that she was letting him inside.

Tip grabbed his phone and called Tommy to let him know that tonight was the night.

She knew that she couldn't hold him off much longer without him knowing that something was up. With a smile she whispered, "Come inside."

"My pleasure." He smiled and followed her inside.

Both smiling but both hiding a secret agenda, they entered the house, not knowing what the night would bring.

Chapter Twenty-four

Game Time

"Let's go merk this nigga," Tommy said to Tip outside of Diamond's house. He'd been waiting for this day and couldn't wait to get it over with. He wanted to get on with his life with Diamond and not have guards constantly following her around. Chance was a constant reminder of a night that he wanted her to forget.

"Let's do it," Tip said, retrieving his gun from his waist.

Using the key that Diamond gave him, they quietly entered the house and made sure that the door closed behind them without making a sound. Tommy gave directions with hand motions. They moved through the house like snipers, checking around every corner before entering the next room.

Diamond and Chance had retreated to her bedroom, where she was in the bathroom and he was patiently waiting on the bed. Tommy and Tip crept up the steps and made their way down the hall toward the room. They stopped just short of the door, which was left open. They could hear Diamond talking to Chance through the door. Tommy nodded, giving Tip the cue. Both men walked into the room and began pumping bullets into an unsuspecting Chance. His body jerked as each bullet pierced his body in different spots. Blood splattered all over the walls, bed, floor, and other exposed surfaces.

Diamond sat on the floor in the bathroom with her hands covering both ears, trying to block out the noise.

Tip stopped shooting once Tommy stopped and put his hand in the air.

"Diamond," he yelled as he made his way to the bathroom.

She was still crouched in the corner with her eyes closed and her ears covered.

He bent down in front of her and touched her leg, startling her. "It's okay, babe, everything is okay."

She reached out and hugged him.

"Come on, let me get you out of here," he said.

"I can't go out there, Tommy. I can't. I will see Black and Dior. I just can't." She shook her head and cried.

"Just keep your eyes closed. I promise you won't see a thing," he said, holding her close. He walked her out of the bathroom and out of the room. "Go get in your car and go to my house, okay? I will be there soon, I already have someone outside waiting to follow you there."

"Okay," she said as tears began to fall from her eyes.

"Baby, it's over, okay? It's all over," he said, grabbing the sides of her face and kissing her tears away. "Just go get in the car. I will be there soon."

She did as she was told and made her way to her car to leave.

Tommy returned to the room where Tip was already wrapping Chance's body up in the bed linens. "Did you call them to come clean this shit up?" he asked.

"Yeah, this will be all cleared away in the next two hours," Tip replied.

"All right, I'm gonna go home and get her together. Call me when this shit is done."

"All right."

Tommy left the house and made his way home to meet Diamond. Once he arrived he found her balled up on the sofa in the dark. He knew that it would take some time before she was comfortable again, but he would work as hard as he could to make sure that happened. He set his gun down on the table and walked over to her. Without saying a word, he hugged her and cradled her face as she cried.

"I got you now, and I'm keeping my promise to Black. I will handle you with care," he whispered in her ear before leaning his head back onto the back of the chair and closing his eyes. He truly believed that Black would be looking down on them, satisfied with the way that he handled things. If there was anything that he could have done differently, he'd want Black here by his side, but he knew with Black here, Diamond could never be his. He'd worked hard to keep her unharmed and now that he had her he didn't plan on letting her go. "I love you, Diamond," he whispered.

"I love you too," she replied, finally letting him know that the feelings were mutual.

Chapter Twenty-five

The Culprit

Alisha sat, looking out of the hospital room's window with many thoughts running through her mind. She was saddened thinking about the events that led them to the place where they currently were. Just a few weeks earlier she and Lucky were out shopping and shooting the breeze; now she lay clinging on to life. She was frustrated because she'd tried her best to steer her away from a life with a criminal, fearing that she'd end up exactly where she had. Thinking back, Lucky was always drawn to the rough, street type and every relationship led to a horrible ending. Every so often she'd look over at Lucky and then back out of the window when she hadn't noticed a change. Though the prognosis wasn't good she was optimistic. One thing that rang true about her best friend was the fight in her, and she'd always managed to pull herself through any circumstance. After standing and peering out of the window for ten minutes, she walked over to the bedside and grabbed a hold of Lucky's hand before saying a silent prayer with her eyes closed. As usual she held her friend's hand tightly, but unlike any other time before then she felt a twitch in her hand. She immediately opened her eyes and looked at Lucky.

"Lucky?" she called out.

Lucky's eyes began to flutter as she fought to see the face behind the voice that was so familiar to her.

Alisha was now standing and calling her name over and over, hoping that it would bring her around. "Nurse," she called frantically from Lucky's beside. She was afraid to move from the room for fear that Lucky'd fall back into the deep sleep where she'd been since being shot. "Nurse! I need a nurse in here," she yelled and pressed the red call bell located on the wall. She continued to yell for what seemed like forever until a nurse entered the room.

"She's waking up," she yelled at the nurse who came over to the side of the bed, checked the monitor which displayed Lucky's vital signs, and walked out into the hallway to call a doctor.

Alisha backed into the corner of the room while the doctor entered the room to see if she could be removed from the ventilator, which had kept her alive the past few weeks.

"Ma'am, we're going to have to ask you to sit out in the waiting area while they evaluate her," the female nurse said, gently pushing Alisha out of the room.

Alisha looked on but obeyed the nurse's command, as she didn't want to interfere with anything that could bring her best friend back. She grabbed her bag and walked out of the room, looking back one last time at the crowd of medical staff, which now surrounded Lucky's bedside. She walked out in the hallway with her stomach full of butterflies. She could barely stay still as she attempted to sit in the waiting room. She paced the floor for what seemed like an hour before the nurse came out to the waiting area to get her.

"What happened? Is she okay?" Alisha said, rushing over to the nurse.

"Yes, she's fine. She is asking for you. She's also asking for someone by the name of Chance. Do you know how to reach him or her?"

Alisha stood silent for a few moments, not sure what to say. She dreaded the moment that she'd have to tell Lucky that Chance had been murdered. She let out a sigh before responding to the nurse, who now stood with a look of confusion on her face.

"Actually, he was killed and I really don't know how I'm going to break the news to her."

"Well, maybe you should wait you know. It probably isn't the best time to share that sort of news with her. I'd say let her get out the woods before dropping the bomb."

"Okay, can I see her now?"

"Sure, I'll walk you back."

Alisha walked into the room with a huge smile on her face. She was excited to see her but she was also nervous because she knew Lucky wouldn't rest until she saw Chance. She knew it would be even more difficult once she learned that she was carrying his child. Luckily the trauma hadn't terminated the pregnancy and with the help of medication and life support the baby was actually doing well.

"There's my best friend." Lucky's face lit up when she saw Alisha enter the doorway.

"Girl, I am so damn happy to see your eyes. You just don't know," she said, walking over to the bed right into Lucky's opened arms.

"Girl, what the hell happened?" Lucky asked, still unsure about the events that led her to the hospital.

"You were shot, girl. I thought I lost you. I couldn't have that. What the hell would my life be without you?" She laughed and sat down on the stool next to the bed.

"Boring as all hell." She laughed. "Have you seen Chance? I really need to talk to him. I know he's probably out working like the workaholic he is." She smiled.

"No, actually I haven't seen him, but I can try to contact him for you."

"Great, girl, because they just told me that I'm pregnant! I know he'll be so happy. I wasn't ready for kids just yet but, hey, God has His own plan." She smiled and rubbed her hands across her belly.

"I know, they told me when they bought you in. I'm happy for you, I really am. I'm just glad that you are awake." She struggled to hold back tears, as she wanted to tell her that her unborn child's father would never hear the good news. She decided that she'd leave and allow her to rest. This way she could figure out how and when she'd break the news to her.

"Well, I'm going to let you get some rest, girl. The nurses have my number if anything goes down, but I will be back first thing in the morning to see you, okay?"

"Promise?"

"I promise, girl." She leaned in to hug her before turning her back and leaving the room.

Lucky sat there, wondering where Chance was and why he hadn't been by her bedside when she opened her eyes. She decided not to worry herself with it that evening and soon she drifted off to sleep.

The following morning she was allowed to use the phone and she dialed his phone only to find that the number was no longer in service. An hour later Alisha walked through the door with flowers and a huge teddy bear.

"Hey, girl, here as promised with a little friend," she said, setting the flowers down on the counter.

"I called Chance and his number is disconnected. What's going on with him, Alisha? He's not breaking up with me is he?" she said with her face full of sadness. Dry tears were on both sides of her face. It would break her heart if he'd walked out on her, especially when she needed him the most.

Alisha sat down on the stool and looked down at the floor. She knew that it was inevitable and she was going to have to tell her regardless of the nurse's advice. She couldn't leave her out in the dark any longer.

"What is it, Alisha? Please be honest with me," she pleaded.

"Look, you know I love you and I never want to see you hurting."

"Just spill it already, Alisha." She raised her voice. She wanted to know what it was regardless of how it would feel.

"He's dead," she said after a short sigh.

"What?" She sat up in bed. "That's a joke, right? No way he's really dead, Alisha."

"I'm sorry, Lucky, but it's not a joke. He was murdered. Shot over ten times."

"Noooooooooooooooooooo," she screamed in agony. She had prepared herself for something else. She thought for sure he'd left her for another woman, but never dead. It had never crossed her mind as one of the reasons why she didn't see him when she opened her eyes. Her body was aching and tears began to pour from her eyes.

Alisha hugged Lucky and let her tears fill her shoulder. She felt her pain and she knew that the news would be devastating. She wished that it was really a cruel joke and Chance would come walking through the door, but she was there at his funeral so she knew for certain that it would never happen.

"Who killed him? Do they even know?" she asked, pulling herself away from Alisha.

"They do know but they haven't told me. I told Romeo you were awake and he said he would come talk to you."

"I can't believe this. Why him? He was everything that I needed in a man. Now I'm going to have to raise this baby alone." She continued to cry.

"You're a fighter, Lucky, and I know you'll get through this. I'm here for you. Anything that you need."

"I don't know what to do. I can't understand this, I just can't."

Alisha reached in to hug her again. The two hugged until they heard a knock at the door. Lucky sat up and quickly tried to wipe the remnants of sorrow from her face.

"Hey, I came as soon as I heard," Romeo said with a letter and flowers. He set the flowers down and handed Lucky the envelope.

"Aww thanks, Romeo. What's this?" she asked, waving the envelope in the air.

"It's from Chance. He told me to give it to you if anything ever happened to him. Sorry that I had to deliver it. I'd rather it be him to speak to you instead."

"Do you know what happened? I mean how did this happen to him?"

"Yeah, I know what happened and believe me, we're going to take care of it. I don't want you to worry about that though. I just want you to get well and worry about that baby you're carrying. He wouldn't want it any other way."

"I just . . . I just . . ." she stuttered.

"I know, believe me. He was my best friend. Killed me to bury him. I wanted to go kill everybody, literally."

"I just don't know what I'm going to do. I have nothing. I left everything to be with him."

"Don't worry about that. You'll be taken care of. His house, I'll have it signed over to you, and also the money that he had put up for something like this. I don't want you to stress about anything. You're family to me because he was like my brother and he loved you to pieces."

"I know he did. I just can't believe that I won't see his face again. I miss him so much already."

"Well again, I don't want you to worry. I'm gonna roll out to handle some business but I wanted to make sure you got that letter. Here's the key to his house. Call me when they are discharging you so I can come by to make sure everything is good at the crib." He passed her a small key chain with two keys on it.

"Thanks a lot, Romeo. I appreciate you coming."

"No problem. Get well soon, all right?" he said before leaving the room.

"I'm almost afraid to read this letter," she said, looking down at the white envelope.

"Well, I can give you some privacy if you want me to," Alisha said, placing her hand on top of Lucky's hand.

"No, you don't have to leave. Really, I want you to stay. Who knows what the hell is in this letter. I want you here as a shoulder to cry on if I need one." She laughed.

"Well, let's do it," Alisha replied with a smile.

Lucky took a deep breath before flipping the envelope over to the back and tearing it open. She was anxious but nervous at the same time. She pulled out a single sheet of paper with a handwritten note that read:

> Dear Lucky,
> If you're reading this, it's most likely because I am no longer here to tell you how I feel. When I came home from prison I looked forward to returning to my life the way that it was. My home, my business, my child, and my wife were all that kept me going while I was away. When I came home and realized that nothing was the same it was a hard pill to swallow. I didn't know how to handle it. All I could think about was getting back on top, getting my life back, minus the conniving woman I married. I had no intention of jumping into a relationship but then I met you. You were truly a breath of fresh air and I can honestly admit for the first time in my life, I was head over heels for a woman. When I met you, I vowed to take you away from the life that you lived. I

wanted to see you blossom into the woman you were meant to be. I know how much you care for me and I know that it's breaking your heart right now to be without me. I want you to know that I'm sorry. I'm sorry for any pain that this will cause you because one thing that I never planned to do is hurt you.

I'm sitting here now writing this letter knowing that what I am about to do could lead to my death in the end but I need to gather the things that belong to me. I want to get the things that I need to give you the life that I want to provide. One thing that I want you to know, which, if you're reading this, you probably already know, is that you never have to worry about money or a place to live because everything that I have is yours. I know that none of what I am saying will ever take the place of me being there with you but I want you to know that I am sorry. I never wanted to cause you any pain and regardless of how things may seem I love you. I want you to make sure that you finish school and use the money that Romeo provides wisely. I know you're a smart girl so I trust that you will.

Well, I'm going to end this letter with this. If things had turned out different, I'd be asking you to marry me and become the mother of my child. I love you, Lucky, with all of my heart.

Reed

Tears flowed out of her eyes as she took the letter and neatly placed it back inside of the envelope.

"How could you?" she said aloud. "If you loved me why would you leave me here alone? Why would you leave us alone?" she said, rubbing her stomach. She had a lot to figure out and there wasn't any amount of money that could take the place of a father. She hated the fact that she was going to have to raise their child alone. Her child would never know the amazing man she fell in love with.

The more she thought about it, the angrier she got. She wanted to know who the culprit was. She needed to know just like she needed air to breath. She wanted them to pay for what they'd done and taking Romeo's word wasn't going to be enough. Their heads on a platter would be the only things that could suffice for the pain that she felt.

Alisha sat next to Lucky, silent. She knew that her friend would never be the same. She didn't know anything that she could say at that moment that could make her feel any better.

Finally, after a few minutes more of crying, Lucky wiped her face and looked at Alisha. "I need you to get Romeo on the phone," she said with a sharp, even tone.

"Okay," Alisha replied, knowing that she meant business. Alisha pulled her cell phone out of her bag and dialed the number that Romeo gave her. The phone rang twice before a deep male voice boomed through the receiver.

"What's wrong?" he said, wondering if things with Lucky had suddenly turned bad.

"Lucky wants to speak to you," she replied before passing Lucky the phone.

"I read the letter and I just want you to know that I appreciate all that you have done and will do for me, however, it doesn't change the fact that my child will now be born without a father. I need them to pay, Romeo. Do you hear me? I need their family to feel the pain that I'm feeling at this very moment."

"I got you, Lucky. I have everything under control, okay? If you know anything about Chance you know that he wouldn't trust me with his assets if he didn't think that I would do the right thing. Trust me, okay? He was like my brother, I told you this. Just worry about you and that baby getting well and I will see you when you get home."

She paused before responding, hoping that he was as trustworthy as he appeared. "Okay, I will see you soon," she replied.

"What did he say?" Alisha asked anxiously.

"He says that he has it all under control."

"Do you believe him?"

"What other choice do I have, Alisha?"

"Well, I guess you're right. Well, I'm going to go and let you rest. I will see you first thing in the morning okay?"

"Okay. Thanks for coming, girl," Lucky replied before reaching out to hug Alisha.

"No problem," she said before leaving the room.

Lucky leaned back on the bed and turned her head toward the window. With the letter still in her hand she placed it close to her chest and hugged it tightly. The scent of his cologne could still be smelled on the outside of the envelope and the scent was just enough to soothe her until she could fall asleep, confident that his soul was with her and that everything would truly be okay.

"I love you too," she whispered before drifting off to sleep.

Chapter Twenty-six

Finale

"I have a gift for you," Romeo said, walking into the living room as Lucky sat on the sofa, watching TV.

Six months had passed since she was released from the hospital and her due date was approaching quickly. She hadn't been outside much as she didn't feel comfortable with her present shape and situation. Luckily, Romeo had stepped up and been there for her just as promised.

"A gift for me? Why do you keep spoiling me, Romeo?" She smiled.

"I'm trying to cheer you up. I don't want you sitting around here all miserable and shit. It's a lot out there that you can be doing you know. I told you I took care of everything so you don't have to ever worry about those niggas in the street. I'll be damned if I'd let any muthafucker hurt someone I care about," he said, holding a small box behind his back.

"You care about? You care about me?" she asked, surprised by the last comment.

"Come on now, you know I care about you. Why else would I be here every day?"

"Because you promised Chance," she replied.

"No, I promised him that I'd see to it that you were taken care of. I didn't promise to be here with you every day." He laughed.

"Well, I guess that I care about you too, Romeo."

"You guess? Well shit, I might as well walk back out with my gift then, shit." He began to back away toward the door.

"I'm just joking." She laughed. Up until this point she never knew how he felt about her so she hadn't really thought about revealing her own feelings for him. Naturally, when you spend time with someone you gain feelings, especially when they bend over backward to make sure that you're happy. She could see why he and Chance had been such good friends, because he resembled him. He reminded her of the things in Chance that she fell in love with. "Now can I have my gift already?" She laughed while holding her hand out.

"You still haven't said that you care about me, Lucky." He stood still.

"Yes, Romeo, I care about you and I mean that from the bottom of my heart."

He smiled, showing all of his pearly whites before walking over to the sofa and sitting down. "All right, here," he said, putting the small box into her open hand.

The small white box was decorated with a teal-blue bow. She gently untied the bow and lifted the top off of it to find a small ring box inside. She looked up at him, confused.

"What?" he asked.

"What is this, Romeo?"

"Just open it and see," he replied with a smile.

She pulled the ring box out of the box and slowly opened it, revealing a platinum ring with a huge five-karat pink diamond in the center.

"Before you say anything let me tell you what it's for. Before Reed died, around the same time that he gave me that letter for you, he gave me this ring to hold. He told me that if anything happened to him to wait until this day and give it to you. He was going to ask you to marry him with this ring, on this day, his mother's birthday. Now, he truly believed that on this day, I would care about you and he also told me that he wouldn't want or trust any man to be with you except me. At first, I was confused, believe me. I looked at him liked he'd lost his mind. At the time, I thought for sure he was talking crazy and he would be here to give it to you himself. I also thought in the event that he wasn't here, I'd never be comfortable loving the same woman he did, even with his blessing. However, regardless of the way I felt that day, I do care about you and I do love you, Lucky. This ring is his blessing. It's his way of letting you know that it's okay to care about me, and it's okay to love me. I'm not asking you to marry me, Lucky, but what I am asking is that you let your guard down and let me in. I promise that I will be here for you and the baby. The baby will never want for a father because I will be all the father he needs." He paused to wipe the tears from her face. "Can you do that for me?"

She sat there stunned and relieved at the same time. She never wanted to do anything that would disrespect his memory. Knowing that he wanted her to move on and be happy relaxed her mind and made her heart smile. She looked down at the ring and looked back at Romeo, who was sitting silent, waiting for her to respond. She wasn't going to fight any longer. She wanted to be happy and she truly believed that Romeo was more than capable of keeping her that way.

"Can you help me put it on?" she asked, breaking the silence.

He smiled and grabbed the ring box before pulling the ring off the holder and placing it on her finger. As he slid the ring on, she grabbed his hands and moved in and kissed him. He gently grabbed both sides of her face and took control of the kiss, doing what he'd wanted to do for so long. After a few seconds they separated and stared at each other.

"So what does this mean?" he asked.

"I guess this is your lucky day because I'm going to give you the chance that you're asking for." She smiled and looked down at the ring that glistened on her finger.

"You've just made me a very happy man," he replied before leaning in to kiss her again.

The two got comfortable on the sofa as she lay in his arms and continued watching television. This evening, both of them had a lot to look forward to, with the blessing of Chance. Finally, she could look forward to her future and a happily-ever-after. Even if that wasn't possible she was going to look forward to it.

Chapter Twenty-seven

Life After Black

"Do you, Thomas, take Diamond to have and to hold from this day forward, for better or for worse, for richer, for poorer, in sickness and in health, to love and to cherish, from this day forward until death do you part?" Reverend Brooks asked, holding his Bible in his hand.

"I do." Tommy smiled.

"And do you, Diamond, take Thomas to have and to hold from this day forward, for better or for worse, for richer, for poorer, in sickness and in health, to love and to cherish, from this day forward until death do you part?"

"I do," Diamond spoke loudly.

"By the powers vested in me, I now pronounce you husband and wife. You may now kiss your bride."

Tommy moved close and planted a kiss on Diamond's lips.

"Ladies and gentlemen, I present to you Mr. and Mrs. Thomas Jones."

The guests in attendance all stood up from their seats and began to clap. Diamond and Tommy smiled as they began their walk up the aisle and out of the church. At that moment Diamond couldn't imagine her life being any different. Looking back, she wondered why things had turned out the way that they had but at this moment, she was the happiest woman in the world. She had a loving husband and a bun in the oven. Her baby Dior would never be replaced, nor would the love that she had for Black; however, her new family was making life worth living. She'd wanted to give up more times than she could count, but she realized that things happened for a reason and if it were meant for her to die she'd be dead by this point.

"Can you believe it? We're married. Wow. I never thought I'd be standing here," Tommy said with a huge smile on his face as he held Diamond close.

"I never would've imagined this would be my life but I'm glad that it is. I love you, Tommy, more than you'll ever know."

"Well, you'll have the rest of our lives to show me," he replied.

The two made their way over to the reception hall after taking photos with their wedding party. Things couldn't be more perfect. The evening went off without a hitch and Diamond was smiling from ear to ear. Once the evening was over they retreated to their house to gather their things and prepare for their honeymoon.

"Where did this come from?" Diamond asked, noticing a small envelope on their coffee table.

"I don't know, maybe one of the guests. Open it and see," he said as he walked out of the living room, into the kitchen.

Diamond grabbed the envelope and sat down on the sofa before flipping it over and ripping it open. Inside was a card, which read "Congrats to the bride and groom" on the front. Once opened, she closed her eyes and hoped that what she read was somehow totally different than what was really written. Tears flowed from her eyes as she tried to figure out what she'd done to be in this position yet again.

Tommy entered the room after hearing her sobbing. "What's wrong, babe? What is it?" he asked, sitting down on the side of her.

"It says, 'you took everything from me. Don't think you'll live happily ever after.'"

Tommy snatched the card from her and read it again. Anger filled his veins as he'd covered all ends to make sure that this night would be perfect. Now, instead of ending the night on a high note he had to figure out who the hell sent the card and what the hell they had planned. He grabbed his wife and cradled her in his arms. He wanted to make her feel safe just like she had in the past.

"Don't worry about anything. Whoever sent this is going to be taken care of. You hear me?" he asked.

"Yes, Tommy, I hear you," she replied. She wasn't sure if she believed him but she didn't have any other choice but to depend on his protection. She looked down at her round belly and began to rub it. Since Tommy had gone to great lengths in the past to save her she hoped that he'd go even further to protect his seed. She closed her eyes and rested in his arms while saying a silent prayer that things would be okay.

ORDER FORM
URBAN BOOKS, LLC
97 N18th Street
Wyandanch, NY 11798

Name (please print):_____

Address:_____

City/State:_____

Zip:_____

QTY	TITLES	PRICE
	16 On The Block	$14.95
	A Girl From Flint	$14.95
	A Pimp's Life	$14.95
	Baltimore Chronicles	$14.95
	Baltimore Chronicles 2	$14.95
	Betrayal	$14.95
	Black Diamond	$14.95

Shipping and handling: add $3.50 for 1st book, then $1.75 for each additional book.

Please send a check payable to:

Urban Books, LLC

Please allow 4-6 weeks for delivery

ORDER FORM
URBAN BOOKS, LLC
97 N18th Street
Wyandanch, NY 11798

Name (please print):_____

Address:_____

City/State:_____

Zip:_____

QTY	TITLES	PRICE
	Black Diamond 2	$14.95
	Black Friday	$14.95
	Both Sides Of The Fence	$14.95
	Both Sides Of The Fence 2	$14.95
	California Connection	$14.95
	California Connection 2	$14.95

Shipping and handling: add $3.50 for 1st book, then $1.75 for each additional book.
Please send a check payable to:
Urban Books, LLC
Please allow 4-6 weeks for delivery

ORDER FORM
URBAN BOOKS, LLC
97 N18th Street
Wyandanch, NY 11798

Name (please print):_____

Address:_____

City/State:_____

Zip:_____

QTY	TITLES	PRICE
	Cheesecake And Teardrops	$14.95
	Congratulations	$14.95
	Crazy In Love	$14.95
	Cyber Case	$14.95
	Denim Diaries	$14.95
	Diary Of A Mad First Lady	$14.95
	Diary Of A Stalker	$14.95

Shipping and handling: add $3.50 for 1st book, then $1.75 for each additional book.

Please send a check payable to:

Urban Books, LLC

Please allow 4-6 weeks for delivery

ORDER FORM
URBAN BOOKS, LLC
97 N18th Street
Wyandanch, NY 11798

Name (please print):_____

Address:_____

City/State:_____

Zip:_____

QTY	TITLES	PRICE
	Diary Of A Street Diva	$14.95
	Diary Of A Young Girl	$14.95
	Dirty Money	$14.95
	Dirty To The Grave	$14.95
	Gunz And Roses	$14.95
	Happily Ever Now	$14.95
	Hell Has No Fury	$14.95

Shipping and handling: add $3.50 for 1st book, then $1.75 for each additional book.
Please send a check payable to:
Urban Books, LLC
Please allow 4-6 weeks for delivery